<u>Dedication Page</u>

- To Tina, my loving partner in crime, you always have my back, and you are my biggest supporter. I wouldn't have been able to finish this without you. I love you my sugarbooger.

- To Dylan, Logan, Harper, Tyler, Sean, Dane and Hunter. You have all been my great motivators and I love you all so much.

- To my parents, my support system since day one. You both have helped me become the man I am today. I am forever grateful and I love you both so much.

- To Grandma Girl, you were not only my safe place but my best friend. I miss you so much. Hope you're smiling down from heaven and proud of me. I love you.

Chapter One

In 1850, there lived a man by the name of Charles Jones, he lived in the town of Logan, Tennessee. He was in his early twenties, in the prime of his life. Every woman he met wanted to be with him and every man he knew wanted to be him. He was a very wealthy man, he had his Estate, servants who were paid generously, he had his high-class friends and a number of not so high-class friends. He had everything a man could ever want with the exception of the one thing he wanted the most, someone to share it all with. There were many women he knew that would love to be that special woman in his life, but he didn't love them. He wanted the kind of love that stories were written about, the kind that even after they were no longer on this earth people would still talk about their love.

His father, Thomas Jones, had made the family fortune from real estate and the shipping of goods to ports up and down the coast. He met Charles's mother, Regina, when he was twenty-one. She was the daughter of a cattle rancher in Kentucky, and they began courting shortly after meeting. She was a vibrant nineteen year old woman, she was adventurous and so full of life. They were married a year later and she became pregnant five months later. When Charles was five his mother became pregnant with his future sibling. Sadly, due to a rough and brutal winter, after two months she miscarried the baby. It had taken an emotional toll on her and Thomas. They tried for years to have another baby, but it seemed that it wasn't in God's plan for them.

Thomas, during lengthy transports, would take Charles with him. He would teach him about the shipping routes, navigating by the stars and how to fish. They spent many trips fishing and enjoying life. Sometimes Regina would accompany them and she would cook the fish they caught. The ship's crew loved it when she was aboard the ship because they knew that it meant they would be eating much better than they were used to. Regina was also Charles's teacher when they were out on the open seas. She would teach him to read, she would introduce him to new languages, and she taught him to excel in math. When they were home, Charles would attend school, his teachers were always impressed by his will to learn new things and by the rate he would pick up new lessons. He was a popular young man, and he was always respectful to his peers.

As the years went by Charles began working for his father and was well on his way to becoming his father's business partner. He would take over some of the shipping duties and became well known throughout the ports. He was regarded as a respectable and fair businessman; this made his parents truly proud of him. For his twentieth birthday, his parents threw him a big party. They had hoped he would meet a nice young woman to become his wife and start a family. He did meet someone at the party, but their courting only lasted a few months.

In February of 1850 his parents had passed away. His mother had passed away from consumption and a year later his father passed from smallpox. At the age of 24, he was one of the country's wealthiest men and one of the loneliest. The closest thing he had to a living relative was Edward, one of his servants whose family had worked for his family for years. Edward was 2 years older than Charles, but they were like brothers and there was nobody that Charles trusted more than Edward. Edward had a son named Jacob. Jacob was 9 years old and was motherless. She had passed after contracting smallpox while nursing

Charles's father. Edward and Jacob were the only servants allowed to live in the house with Charles, while the rest of the servants were limited to a smaller house behind the main estate. The servants quarters were bigger and much more spacious than most in the area, it included their own kitchen and living area outside of their rooms. His generosity and respect for those who served him was probably why there were no issues with the others about Edward and his son staying in the main house.

"Edward my friend, I believe it is time." Charles left the statement very vague.

"Time for what? Lunch?" Edward asked with a confused look on his face.

"Hahaha no, though that is a good idea. It's time for me to find a wife. With the exception of you and Jacob, this house is quite lonely. I crave the love of a good woman and for the sound of children of my own running down these halls." Charles stared off in the distance as he imagined the sound of little feet running. "Ready the wagon and inform the staff that we will be leaving for a few days."

"I will get everything ready." Edward rushed to his son to let him know that he would be gone for a few days and to give everyone their orders while he and Charles were away.

Charles was quite excited about his decision. He was hoping to find a love so strong that it would last for an eternity. Little did he know that it would be that and so much more. A love that would haunt him for many years to come.

He began in the neighboring town of Xavier. He met many women and two of them had sparked his interests. One was a 24-year-old by the name of Victoria. She was the daughter of a wealthy businessman and she was very beautiful. The second was a 23-year-old blonde beauty whose name fit her like the beautiful flower she was named after, Rose. Charles made two dates, the first date was with Victoria and the second was with Rose. Both women knew of the other one and their date, so they decided to make it a contest to win Charles's affection.

For the first date with Victoria, they decided on dinner. They ate and talked for hours. While they were talking Charles noticed Victoria was acting strange. He had asked her what was wrong, she said nothing was wrong. He said she seemed anxious, and her reply was that she wasn't anxious, she was just happy. Charles could tell that she was hiding something and that was no way to start a relationship. He thanked her for accompanying him to dinner and said goodnight. Upon returning to his hotel room Charles began to wonder why she seemed so anxious, nervous would have been one thing, but nerves were not what made him end the night. He figured he might as well get some rest for his evening with Rose tomorrow.

While he slept, he dreamt of the most beautiful woman he had ever laid his eyes upon. She was tall, the same height as him, and she had beautiful flowing blonde hair. Her eyes were hazel and enchanting. Her skin was almost as pale as the winter snow. Even though she looked pale, that's what made her so beautiful. He knew he was dreaming but everything seemed so real. From the breeze passing by to the smell of flowers in the air. As Charles was about to approach her, if only to find out the name of such an angel, he was suddenly awakened by Edward.

"Sir, it's time to get up and begin your day"

"Oh Edward, why did you wake me? I finally found her." Charles sleepily spoke to Edward.

"Found who? You were sound asleep?" Edward was quite confused.

"The woman that I will marry." He blurted out as he sat up. "She was an angel, my friend. And I must find her. Cancel my evening plans with Rose. After breakfast we shall begin our search for her."

"Right away sir." Edward was very confused but did as Charles had instructed. He sent a message to Rose that something had come up, and he had to cancel their date. He readied the carriage and as soon as Charles finished breakfast, they would set off to find his bride that he dreamt of.

"We will head to the town of Wills first, then to Brooks and continue from there." He couldn't get the woman from his dreams out of his head, nor did he want to. He wanted so badly to find her that he barely finished his food and was already getting his stuff together so that they may leave promptly. And as they left the town of Xavier, Charles was filled with excitement. There was also a strange strong feeling in his gut that something was about to happen, but he dismissed the feeling as excitement.

When they reached the edge of the town, Edward called back to Charles to inform him that they had arrived. As the carriage made its way through town Charles noticed that something was very wrong. The town was like a cemetery, nobody walking the streets and no sounds at all.

"What in God's name is going on here? The town is as quiet as a graveyard. Where is everyone?" Charles asked as a feeling of dread in his stomach began to grow.

"I don't know, maybe they are all in the church or the saloon." Edward answered Charles with a hint of fear in his voice.

" A whole town, in the church, in the middle of the day? I highly doubt that. You would hear music from the church or the preacher's voice. Even the saloon is filled with quietness." The uneasy quietness of the town was enough to scare any man. " Go and check the church and the saloon for the townspeople. And hurry up, I don't want to be here any longer than we have to be." Charles was beginning to fear the worst because of the quietness of the town. He felt fear and anxiousness rising from deep down and more than anything he wanted to leave.

Edward headed towards the church first. Glimpsing at the surrounding buildings as he made his way to the doors. He moved to the side of the church to the stained glass window. He pressed his hand to the window to try to see inside. Out of the corner of his eye he thought he saw something moving in the church. It was hard to see through the colored glass, so he decided to head for the main doors. He pushed the doors open and the church let out a stench so putrid that he gagged. After a quick breather he entered the church and stared in horror at the scene in front of him. Before he could call to Charles, something dark flashed in front of him. He began to feel something warm on his shirt. As he looked down, he saw blood. With a wet fluid filled cough, he realized it was his blood. As fast as his feet could take him, he ran to the carriage. Charles had gotten out and was staring at Edward in confusion as he ran towards him. The moment Edward got to the carriage he fell to Charles's feet.

"Edward, get up! What did you see? What happened?" Charles frantically turned over his friend and what he saw was a blow to his heart. Edward had four deep gauges angling from his neck to chest. The gauges looked like claw marks, as if he had been attacked by an animal. Edward coughed up a mouthful of blood, grabbed Charles's arm and said Jacob. After that last and final word, his head moved slightly and his eyes were lifeless. Charles knew that his friend was dead. " I will look after Jacob, my friend. Goodbye." Charles closed Edward's eyes and rose to his feet. Now filled with fear, anger, sadness and curiosity, he grabbed a gun from the carriage and made his way to the church.

As he got close to the open doors of the church he could smell something horrible. He could only describe it as the smell of death. As he got closer, the smell intensified and almost made him throw up. Moving up the stairs to the entrance, he covered his nose with one hand and held the gun tight in his other hand. The rotting stench proved to be too much for him, Charles leaned over and threw up everything he had eaten for breakfast. He wiped his mouth with his sleeve and stood up. He took no more than three steps into the church and he was frozen in horror. The smell was from the rotting corpses of townspeople. Blood covered the floor, the seats of the church and the walls were even stained with blood splatter. There were at least twenty people in the church and all had been brutally slaughtered. It was like a savage animal had torn through them. Charles trembled in fear as he gazed at the bodies, which were torn apart. What made him run out the church faster than he had ever ran before was what he saw on the preacher's podium. Bible pages had been ripped through and blood soaked and placed on top of them was the preacher's head. Fear was frozen on the face of the preacher. Backing up to the door, slowly making sure he did not trip over the bodies he had stepped over, something moved. Charles stopped for a second, only to see a shadow in the corner of the church and then he took off. Hauling ass back to the carriage, Charles jumped over his fallen friend and reached for the reins and snapped the horses.

He didn't slow down for anything, and he worked the horses harder than ever. When he finally arrived in Brooks the horses had been worked to exhaustion. Charles, himself was barely able to get off the carriage without falling. He quickly got to his feet, after almost landing on his face, and ran to the sheriff's office. Bursting through the door, he began rambling about what had happened. He was talking so fast that the sheriff had no idea as to what he was saying. He tried his best to calm the frantic Charles down but had no luck. He led him to the hotel across from his office and got Charles a room so he could calm down somewhere safe. He told him they would talk after he got some rest and was calm.

Throughout the night Charles had nightmares about the church and the shadowy figure he had seen. Even though he was asleep he had the strangest feeling that he was being watched. One of the dreams was of his driver Edward and him dying again. Only this time he arose as something very feral and dangerous. He chased him into the church where he tripped over dismembered corpses. Charles ran as fast as he could but he felt as if he was running through sand. The dream ended as Edward was about to attack him and he fell backwards. Everything had gone dark and then he seen her. Charles was looking at his dream woman. She was walking alone. Even from behind he could recognize her and he recognized the sign she was walking past. It read "Welcome to Brooks". She then turned around to look at him. She was covered in blood, on her hands, the front of her dress and even on her face. She took a step towards him, reaching out for him. He couldn't tell if she was reaching out for help or to grab him. The dream ended so abruptly that he sat up in his room, screaming and gasping for air.

As he tried to regain some sense of awareness and orientation, he noticed he was not alone in his room. There she was, his mysterious beautiful dream woman, sitting on the edge of his bed. She was trying to calm him down and was gently pushing him down. Her pushing somehow helped him regain his equilibrium from the ghastly nightmare. Once he began to calm down, he just stared at her. Looking at her face, clothing, and hands. He saw no trace of the blood that she was covered in from his dream.

"Who are you? What are you doing in my room and how did you get in here?"

"I am a nurse. I arrived early this morning and the sheriff asked me to come up here to check on you. He said you ran into his office like a crazed man and you were ranting and raving about a church and corpses in the next town over. I believe the town was Wills. Is that right?"

"Yes, you are right. My driver Edward was attacked and died right in front of me. He was a good man, His son will be devastated and heartbroken. I went into the church and saw at least twenty people in pieces all over the church. I ran to my carriage and left as fast as I could. As I left, I had the strangest feeling that I was being watched by someone or something. I arrived here last night, scared and frantic, and the sheriff led me here to this room where I passed out from exhaustion. The odd part is last night as I slept, I dreamt of a woman, she was walking this way, and she was covered in blood. Her hands, clothing and face were covered. As she passed the sign to Brooks, she turned around and I swear to god himself that she looked identical to you."

"Me? That is impossible. Firstly, sir, we have never met. And I didn't arrive through Wills. I came in from the other side of town."

"That was not the first time that I had dreamt of you. The day before yesterday I dreamt of you, and I must admit you are much more beautiful in person. And you still have not told me your name."

" I am sorry to hear about your driver's unfortunate death. Especially having died in such a gruesome way. It is truly terrible. Even though you basically asked me if I murdered an entire town, my name is...."

Before she could answer Charles, the sheriff rushed through the doorway. Frantic, like Charles was when he arrived in Brooks, the sheriff said "M.. My n...name is Sheriff Dylan." Charles went over to the sheriff and led him to the chair in the room.

"I'm guessing you went to Brooks to check out my story."

" Yes I did." The sheriff was starting to calm down. "Did you only go into the church? Did you check anywhere else?" Some of the color was returning to the sheriff's face but he was still trembling.

"Yes, I only went into the church. There were at least 20 people ripped to pieces and parts everywhere. But that was the only place I checked, I didn't have the stomach or the nerve to check anywhere else. After my driver came back to the carriage with the bizarre wounds and died, I left as fast as I could. Why? What did you see?" Charles feared the answer.

" I went to Wills this morning. When I arrived I found your driver, I had my men load his body into a casket for his burial. Then I then went into the church and like you said at least 20 people were torn to pieces, all over the place. The smell was worse than anything I have ever smelled before. Then I walked over to the saloon. Thought maybe some whiskey would help the smell go away. As soon as I walked into the saloon." Sheriff Dylan paused for a breath "It had to be the rest of the town. At least 35 people, from what I could count, scattered all over the place. Heads ripped off, arms and legs torn from the bodies. That wasn't the worst part, not by a long shot. Inside a few of the liquor bottles were the eyes and fingers of some of the townspeople. I ran outta that place and we hauled ass back here. God it was awful." Sheriff Dylan walked over to the dresser where there were a couple bottles of whiskey sitting. He grabbed a bottle and took the biggest drink of his life.

Sheriff Dylan left Charles's room with the whiskey bottle in hand. From what he just told them, he clearly needed that bottle more than anyone else.

"I hope I never have to see something so terrible. Those townspeople, all murdered and for what reason. It is truly a horrific tragedy." Pausing to regroup her thoughts. She was going to get up to leave but Charles grabbed her hand. She turned towards him and smiled. "My name is Cassandra." He let her hand slowly fall from his. "I shall be back in a little while to check on you, if that is ok?"

"Yes ma'am that would be quite alright with me." Charles smiled as Cassandra left the room. He only wished Edward was there to meet her.

As he thought of his driver, his friend, he had wondered how he was going to tell Jacob the news of his father's death. He knew the boy would take it very hard, but Charles would take care of him as if he was his own son. Charles went down to the caretaker's office to arrange for Edwards' body to be taken home.

When Cassandra returned Charles had already showered, shaved and was in new clothes. In hand he had flowers for her and was smiling from ear to ear.

"Shouldn't you be resting, after the ordeal from yesterday, I assumed you would be sleeping most of the day." Cassandra smiled at the flowers Charles was holding.

"No ma'am. I am fully rested and waiting for you."

"Why were you waiting for me?"

"Well, I was hoping you would like to have dinner with me." Charles was so nervous that she was going to say no or laugh in his face.

"I would love to have dinner with you."

"I am so happy you said yes. I know today has been a gloomy day, but you have surely brightened my mood. Thank you." Charles was starting to think that even with all the death and carnage something good may actually come from this awful trip.

While at dinner Charles told Cassandra that he had something he had to tell her. "Cassandra, I know we have only just met but when I am around you, I feel like I have everything in the world. My life has been so empty and after meeting you, I feel like I have found what I have been looking for."

For a moment Cassandra just sat there smiling at Charles. He grew nervous with her silence and wondered if maybe he had said too much too soon. She was only quiet for a few seconds but to him it felt like forever.

"Charles, that is the sweetest thing anyone has ever said to me in my life. And to be honest with you, since I first saw you I have not been able to stop thinking about you. Your eyes, your smile and your warmth, they have stayed with me, and I don't want to lose that. You are a sweet, kind and handsome man and as fast as this may seem I feel like I am falling in love with you." Cassandra had gotten a little watery eyed while saying that to Charles.

She had moved closer to him and he reached out for her hand. She placed hers in his palm, palm to palm. They moved closer and in sync and then they kissed. Their hearts raced, heat rose and the passion flared. When they stepped back, they both were smiling from ear to ear.

"Wow. I felt like I was flying like a bird!" Charles was the first to speak after the kiss.

"That was incredible. I have never felt like that before in my life." Cassandra was amazed by Charles's passion.

"Let's enjoy our first dinner together, my beautiful angel. I want to know everything about you. And after dinner maybe we can go for a walk and just enjoy each other's company." Charles couldn't stop thinking about that kiss that they had just shared.

During dinner all they did was stare and smile at each other, there was some talking but mostly smiling. Charles did most of the talking, telling her about his family and his home. Cassandra was very brief about her family, saying that they had passed away when she was younger and that she had recently come over from England. She told him about how she learned about medicine from her aunt before leaving.

They were briefly interrupted by another patron of the restaurant who had asked them if they were recently married because "they were just glowing around each other." Charles wanted to say yes but he wasn't sure how Cassandra would have reacted. As fast as things were moving he didn't want to do anything to push or scare her away. Charles paid for dinner and they were on their way back to the hotel when Charles told her his reason for being in Brooks and Wills. She found it a bit surprising and also kind of romantic.

Once they returned to the hotel, Charles grabbed her hand and said he didn't want the night to end just yet. So, they went for a walk to a nearby lake and with the moon shining so bright, it was perfect. He had grabbed a blanket from the carriage before they had left for their walk and after finding the perfect spot, he laid the blanket down and they sat down.

"It's such a beautiful night. And if you don't mind me saying, with you here it couldn't be any more perfect. I am so happy we met. I wish it was under more pleasant circumstances." Charles was so happy to be sitting there with Cassandra yet he felt awful for having such a great time, especially since Edward had just been murdered.

Cassandra could see it in his eyes, the grief of his friend's death was battling the love he was feeling for her. "I am truly sorry for the loss of your dear friend, and I am sorry if this sounds selfish, but I have never been this happy as I am now with you." She slowly moved her hand to his.

He smiled, squeezed her hand and leaned in to kiss her. "You truly are an angel." He whispered as he pressed his lips to hers. "Cassandra, I think you are the most beautiful, kindest, sweetest and most caring woman I have ever met. I feel like I can accomplish anything when I am with you. I know we don't know much about each other, yet, but I feel as if I can tell you anything and everything." Charles leaned in and kissed Cassandra and they just held each other for a moment before laying on the blanket he had brought with.

After laying under the stars for a couple of hours, they headed back to the Hotel. Charles had wrapped the blanket that they were sitting on around Cassandra, to keep her warm from the night air. They walked closely and hand in hand the entire way back. Neither of them had ever felt anything like what they felt for each other. Once they reached the Hotel, Cassandra wrapped herself in Charles's arms. He squeezed her tight and didn't want to let go.

"I want to see you again tomorrow. How about lunch?" Charles eagerly asked her.

"You will see me tomorrow. But I have my medical duties that I must attend to. I must go with the sheriff to examine the bodies in Wills. I fear it is going to take some time to examine all the bodies. But the moment that we are done for the day, I am all yours." Cassandra smiled seductively when she said that she would be all his.

Charles led her up to his room and she followed close behind. On the way up she took one of the steps wrong and slipped. Charles quickly reached back and caught her before she fell. She twisted her ankle slightly so he moved to the step she was on and he picked her up and carried her up the last few stairs. Once they got into his room he gently laid her down on the bed. She looked so seductive laying on his bed, hair laid spread out on the pillow and her legs were slightly bent and leaning to the left. He laid next to her, with his hand resting lightly on her side, he leaned over and kissed her. It was a long slow deep kiss and it took both of their breath away. He kissed her again, just as passionate but it lasted just a little bit longer. Taking a brief moment to just look into each other's eyes. Cassandra sat up abruptly and stated that she regrettably had to bring their night to an end.

"What's wrong, did I do something to upset you?" Charles asked nervously.

"No, you did nothing wrong, my love. I…. don't think I am ready to consummate our love in that manner. I wish to save myself for the day that I marry. Please understand, I care about you greatly and I love being held in your arms. I have never felt safer than I do when you are holding me. I am so sorry." Cassandra looked down to the floor with embarrassment and a feeling of shame.

"My love, I completely understand and I wish to uphold your beliefs." Charles felt a bit of relief and pride that she was able to control her emotions in such a manner. "Maybe it would be best if we slow our courting down til we are truly ready to move further and are more familiar with each other."

Cassandra looked up and smiled at him. "That sounds absolutely perfect. Thank you for being so understanding. "As much as I do not wish to leave, I must return to my room. I need to sleep a bit before I attend to my medical duties with the sheriff. He has asked me to accompany him to investigate the possible cause of deaths of the townspeople that you and he discovered. To be honest, I am not sure what assistance he believes I will be able to provide but I will do what I can to bring the people of Brooks and your dear friend some type of justice or closure." Cassandra squeezed his hand and smiled at Charles before she stood up to leave for her room.

Charles squoze her hand in return and stood up with her. He stepped towards and kissed her and whispered "I love you" in her ear before she left. She said it back and began walking to the door. Once she had the doorknob in hand she looked down for a moment then ran to Charles's arms and kissed him, long slow and deep.

As she made her way to her room she noticed the sun would soon be coming up. She closed the curtains in her room, climbed into bed and pulled the covers up. She closed her eyes, seeing Charles's smiling face and drifted off to sleep.

Cassandra was awoken by a loud rapid pounding on her door. She called out, "One moment please, I'm not decent." She quickly changed her clothes and rushed to the door. She opened the door with hope that it was Charles knocking at her door, disappointment set in when she saw it was Sheriff Dylan.

"I beg your pardon ma'am, but I was hoping to begin our investigation and close it up as soon as possible. I really would like to put that God awful town behind me and bury those poor souls." Sheriff Dylan was holding his hat in his hands and as he spoke of the town, Cassandra could see him tightening his grip on the brim. "I had hoped we would be dealing with this earlier in the day but I'm guessing you and our guest had a late evening?"

"Not that it's any concern of yours sir, but yes we did share the evening together. I do apologize for the hour, I must have been more tired than I realized. Nevertheless, I am ready to proceed if you are." Cassandra smirked as she spoke to the sheriff. Partly because she was thinking of Charles and also because she was hoping he wouldn't want to continue with the investigation. She wished to be done with the whole ordeal and begin her life with Charles.

"Perhaps just a quick trip to see if we can maybe figure out what happened. Possibly put a who or what is responsible for this horrific tragedy." The sheriff's eyes went to a blank stare as he spoke of the massacre. "Those were some good people and they deserved better. I had a few friends there." Now on the verge of tears, he continued. "We would drink and play cards in that saloon. Now, my only memory of them will be seeing them in pieces all over that God forsaken town." With weakened knees, the sheriff grabbed the door frame to keep himself from collapsing to the floor.

Cassandra quickly grabbed the sheriff's arms to help steady him on his feet. "Please come in and sit down before you fall and hurt yourself. I will bring you a glass of water." Cassandra quickly moved a chair closer to the Sheriff and handed him the water. "From your account and Charles's description of what happened and the descriptions of the condition of the remains. I would conclude that a wild, crazed animal must have done the killing. Perhaps a deranged bear made its way into the town and……"

The sheriff abruptly interrupted Cassandra. "There's no way in hell that was the work of some damn animal. The way the limbs were placed and parts put into bottles. This was done by some band of maniacs." Face red and out of breath, the sheriff continued. "Maybe this isn't the best idea to have you come along with us ma'am. No disrespect intended but this type of brutality isn't meant for a woman to see. I wouldn't be able to forgive myself if something were to happen to you in that town." The sheriff had made his way to his feet and headed out the doorway. He stopped long enough to tip his hat and say goodbye.

Cassandra closed the door and sighed in relief. She felt bad for letting the sheriff continue to investigate on his own but after all she had heard from both gentlemen, she wished to stay as far from the town of Wills as possible. Her intentions may have been more on the side of selfishness because she was hoping to hear from her love soon. She couldn't get him and his kisses out of her head and with each thought of him her heart felt so happy.

As for Sheriff Dylan, he was anything but happy. He had enlisted the assistance of the local caretaker and his staff to travel with him to Wills. He warned them that the sights that they were about to see were truly the stuff of nightmares. The caretaker suggested a mass grave site for the townspeople of Wills. He said there would be no proper way to bury that many people in individual graves and still ensure that each limb belonged to that person in their grave. With the exception of Edward, Charles's driver, everyone else would be together. A town buried with a large marker listing as many names as they could get from the town's sheriff's office.

They arrived as the sun was beginning to set. Quickly they found Edward's casket and loaded it into the wagon. The town had already started to smell of death and rotting corpses. There was an uneasy feeling as they made their way through town. A member of the caretaker's staff dropped to his knees and gagged from the smell in the air. As they got closer to the saloon the smell only intensified and was near unbearable. Upon entering the saloon flies and maggots were already feasting on the mangled corpses and torn limbs. The blood-soaked wooden floors had a deep red sheen that reflected the lanterns' lights.

The caretaker was the first to speak as he surveyed the carnage "Dear god. What could have done such a horrific thing to these poor souls? I have never seen anything like this. It is monstrous, it is unfathomable. Sheriff, I don't think we should stay here any longer than absolutely necessary. Something is truly amiss here."

"I agree with you completely sir. As much as it pains me to say, I think maybe we should just set the saloon and church aflame. There is no way" Sheriff Dylan stopped speaking and just stared past the church. As he was speaking to the caretaker he had a strange feeling that something was watching them. "My apologies, I thought I saw something in the distance there past the church. I think we should just leave with the driver after we light the church and the saloon ablaze. There is enough whiskey in that saloon to keep the fire going through the night and well into tomorrow.

The caretaker had his crew grab some brush and placed it in the doorway of both buildings. They lit the torches and made their way to both buildings. As they figured, when the torch was thrown into the saloon, the fire spread like a wave. Flames moved up the walls like they knew their purpose. As the crew made their way to the church, there was thickness in the air. They moved briskly, because they didn't want to spend a moment longer than necessary in the town. The moment they reached the steps of the church they were filled with a deep spine tingling fear. The two men were frozen in fear as they saw something moving in the church. They called out for the sheriff and the caretaker to come quickly.

"What is it? What do you see?" The sheriff was in a full sprint with the caretaker close behind.

Both men stopped instantly, as they saw what the men saw. Something both animal-like but looked like a person. The creature was hunched over in the church and was licking the blood off of the limb of one of the townspeople. The sheriff grabbed his pistol, fired a shot at the creature but missed hitting a knocked over pew. The creature growled in anger and turned towards the men nearest to the door. It charged at them at a speed that was faster than either the sheriff or caretaker had ever seen. It blew past the two crew members and vanished into the night. Both men fell to the ground and remained there as the sheriff and caretaker rushed to them. Like Charles's driver Edward, both men had large horrible gauges and they laid on the ground lifeless in a pool of blood.

Sheriff Dylan looked at the caretaker in fear and disbelief. "I am truly sorry for the loss of your men. Please help me carry them to the wagon. Once they are aboard we will set fire to this unholy place and leave this town."

"These men have no families to mourn them. We will put them in the church with the townspeople, and this will be their tomb." The caretaker helped the sheriff lift the two men and put their bodies in the church. The sheriff handed him the torch, and he threw it onto the brush near his men. "Sheriff, what the hell did we just see? What killed these men and this town?" The caretaker was still in shock over the events they had just witnessed. "Have you ever seen anything move like that?"

"I have no idea what we just saw. I couldn't tell if it was an animal or a man. The quickness of it was unreal. I am thankful that we are leaving this town alive. Once we return, there will be a bottle of whiskey for each of us to hopefully help us forget this night." Sheriff Dylan was feeling a mix of emotions. He was happy to be alive, fearful of the creature that they had seen, remorseful for the loss of the caretaker's men and he truly wished to forget this night.

As they drank, both men agreed to never speak of Wills and the creature they had seen. Not even to Charles, whose driver was to be returned to him to take home to bury. If he asks, all they will say is that they burned the saloon and church as a massive tomb for the townspeople of Wills. Both men drank the rest of the night away, the drank to the men and townspeople lost and to their pact.

In the morning, Sheriff Dylan sluggishly went to Charles's room and gave him the news that his driver was in the caretaker funeral parlor. He informed him of the burning of the saloon and church. "Sir, I hope you and Miss Cassandra have a happy life together. If our paths cross again, you will be welcomed here but I do suggest avoiding Wills. Honestly, I would forget that the Town of Wills ever existed. I wish you the best and safe travels." The Sheriff shook Charles's hand and left.

Charles made the arrangements to have his dear friend sent home and buried. Charles invited Cassandra to his home where, if she chose to, she would make his home their home and start a life together.

"Cassandra my love, nothing would please me more than to wake up every morning next to you and go to sleep every night with you in my arms. What I am trying to ask is, Will you marry me and be my wife? Will you allow me to spend every day making you as happy as you make me?" Charles pulled a ring out his pocket and presented it to her as he dropped to one knee.

"Yes. My sweet Charles, I will marry you. And every day I will spend making you as happy as you make me. I am so happy and I love you so much." Cassandra cried tears of joy as Charles placed the ring on her finger and stood up to kiss her. "My dear, I do have a strange request. May we travel in a covered carriage? My fair skin burns quite easily in the sun, and it can be quite painful at times."

"Of course, my love. I will head down and have the carpenters build us one right away. Maybe we can take the more scenic route home. It will take some time to get home but it will give us more time together on our own." Charles knew the "scenic" route would take an extra several days to get home. And that's as if they didn't decide to go anywhere else.

Over the following weeks Charles and Cassandra were drawn closer and got to know each other a lot better. After three months Charles and Cassandra finally returned home to Virginia and got married. The wedding was quite large, family and friends came from all over to partake in the big celebration. When Charles asked Cassandra if he could send invitations to her family, especially her parents, she told him that she had no current living family. She was an only child, and her parents had passed away a few years ago after she had left for her medical schooling. Her parents had never been close to any other parts of the family so she never knew what other relatives she may have had. "It was a lonely childhood, but my parents made sure I never wanted for anything. I miss them dearly." Tears welled up in Cassandra's eyes as she spoke of her parents.

"I am truly sorry for your losses. I do understand the pain of losing your parents. My mother had passed away from consumption and a year later my father passed from smallpox. I am here for you, for whatever you need for as long as we both shall live." He smiled at her with those words and pulled in close and simply held her.

"If it is not too much to ask, my love, can we have the wedding indoors or possibly in the evening under the moon and stars?" She asked Charles.

"Of course, my love. Whatever you want, I will make sure you get." Charles replied as he kissed her hand.

It was after the wedding that strange occurrences began to occur.

Charles noticed that a couple of servants had just gone up and left. It was quite strange because Charles had never had anyone in his service just leave without giving him word first. Rumors were that something had come and stole them in the middle of the night. Others had heard that they left because of the death of Edward. Next, some of the horses and livestock had died in the stable. Charles had the local veterinarian come out to inspect the deceased animals and all they could come up with was that a wolf or wild dog had gotten into the barn, which wasn't entirely unheard of, so Charles made sure the farm hands had access to rifles to protect the rest of the animals.

Then, about ten months after coming home, Cassandra gave birth to a baby girl. They named her Chloe, she had her mother's features, including her gorgeous hazel eyes, blonde hair and her cute little ears. She had Charles's stubbornness even as a baby and she would only fall asleep if she was in his arms. The three of them were the ideal family.

On her first birthday, Charles gave her one of the biggest parties a baby could have. Cassandra said she didn't think it was necessary since Chloe wouldn't remember any of it. But it was his baby girl, and he wanted to celebrate his sweet girl. He even got her a pony, his reasoning was she would ride it once she was older. He even got a horse for Cassandra because he knew how much she enjoyed riding at night when the stars were out and covered the sky like fireflies. As a thank you from his sweet baby girl her first words were "da da." Charles gleamed with pride and love of his sweet baby girl. A couple days later she said "ma ma." They were so happy and proud of their baby girl.

A couple days later Chloe had taken her first steps, and she was walking so much after that. The happy parents could barely get her to sit still after that. The only time she would be still was when she wasn't feeling well. Periodically since she was born, she would get these episodes that lasted roughly a few days when she was sick. Vomiting, fever, chills and she would get deathly pale. Doctors were called each time, but no definite answer was ever given on what was wrong. Eventually Cassandra would tire of all the bickering doctors and send them all away. She'd lock herself in Chloe's room with her daughter and within a day or two they'd come out and Chloe was all smiles and feeling better. This went on for a while.

Three years went by and more servants disappeared, more were hired. Chloe had recently turned 4 and fell ill and it was at its worst. Charles had dozens of doctors come in to examine her, even doctors who practiced unorthodox medicine and none of them could determine what was wrong. Chloe tried to stay strong and always told him "don't worry Daddy I'll be better soon." But she wasn't getting any better. Not even when Cassandra locked them both in Chloe's room, like she always did, when all the doctors had exhausted her patience. Finally, on the day of their wedding anniversary, Cassandra came out of Chloe's room, overcome with tears and anger. The child had died. Their sweet baby Chloe, resting in her bed, pale as fresh fallen snow, was lifeless. She looked so peaceful and not a single ounce of pain in her face. Charles collapsed to the floor at his wife's feet sobbing uncontrollably, unable to bring himself to enter her room. He just laid there, tears soaked and he felt a part of his heart die in that very moment.

After the funeral Cassandra locked herself in Chloe's room refusing to come out because she blamed herself for the child's sickness. Charles just sat in the chair in his room, hours spent staring out the window without speaking a word. They both carried their own grief and feelings of guilt, thinking and wondering if they could have done something more to help their sweet Chloe.

Three weeks had passed. Neither of them had spoken to each other since Chloe's passing. Charles had finally picked himself up and went to go and speak to his wife.

He knocked gently on the door. "Cassandra, my love. Please come out of Chloe's room. I miss you so and I need you my love. I know it has been extremely difficult these past few weeks, but we must come together and be there for each other. I know I want so badly to hold you in my arms." Charles pleaded to his wife.

She did not open the door, but she did speak to him. "I'm so sorry darling. I wish I could bring myself to open this door. I miss you as well but I simply cannot face you right now. This is all my fault."

"How can you blame yourself?" Chales asked his wife. "There was nothing either of us could have done to prevent this and we did everything possible to help our sweet baby. Please Cassandra, do not blame yourself." He was both saddened by his wife's misplaced guilt and confused by her statement.

"My sweet Charles, if you could only understand and realize that there is still so much about me that you do not know. The illness that took our Chloe passed from my blood to hers. It is truly my fault that she's no longer here.

Please husband, just leave me in peace." Cassandra pleaded with Charles to just leave her be.

Charles was confused and heartbroken by his wife's comments. "Cassandra, there was no way you could have carried her illness. You were perfectly healthy when we met and as you are now. Even the many doctors who have seen her over the years were never able to determine a diagnosis. My love, please come out and talk to me." Charles said with tears falling down his reddened cheeks.

"You pay no attention to detail do you husband? Didn't you ever wonder why I never went out during the day or why I eat so little during meals? Does that not make you curious about my habits?" Cassandra cried out in anger as her husband stood in silence

"Yes, it does make me curious but those were your habits, and I only want to make you happy and respect your decisions my dearest. But if it troubles you that I do not ask then, please tell me!"

Charles had a strong feeling he was going to regret asking, but he didn't care about regret. He wanted his wife back and was going to do whatever was necessary.

"Do you really want to know or do you just want to please me?"

"With all my heart I want to know, now will you please tell me?" claimed Charles with some anxiousness in his voice.

And with a deep breath Cassandra opened the door slowly and revealed something that made her husband stare in awe. "This is why I do not go out in the light, why I barely eat when we've had a meal together and why it is my fault our daughter is gone." What she revealed to Charles was easily unnoticeable at first, but when she began talking he practically froze where he was standing. Everything was normal except for two things on her face. One was the look in her eyes, it was the look of someone who had been living for ages and had seen many terrible things. The other was her teeth, two of them on each side of the upper row of teeth, both about a half inch longer than the other teeth and came down to a sharp point. "I am also the reason for the missing servants. Every so often I need fresh blood, so I would take them in the night, drain their blood and bury the body. I am sorry for not telling you before, I was afraid you would leave me. I was afraid you wouldn't love me anymore. I love you and would never do anything to hurt you. This is why our daughter's death is my fault and has been so difficult to move past." Cassandra had started sobbing, her face held in the palm of her hands. Her teeth had shrunk back to their original size.

"Cassandra, my dear, I do wish you would have told me sooner, and this does come as a big surprise to me. The only thing I can think to say is I still love you. It doesn't matter what you have that makes you different. It's you I love. I always have and I always will. Nevertheless, I do not blame you for our daughter's death and neither should you. You couldn't have known that this would happen. She loved you as much as you did her so please take some comfort in that fact." Charles said this while his eyes began to swell with tears from the mix of joy he felt from Cassandra telling him and the upset he felt from not knowing sooner. He tried to comfort his abnormal wife. "I have a question, but I don't want to offend you or sound like a fool."

"Whatever you ask will not offend me. Go ahead with your question." Cassandra started with what seemed like a hint of amusement

"How do you make your teeth grow like that, how does it feel? Most of all, how long have you been able to do that?"

"Firstly, it's called vampirism. My teeth automatically grow when I want them to or when I'm going to "eat" and no, it doesn't hurt when they come down. The feeling of it is amazing because when I get hungry I can hear the heartbeat of whatever the source of my food is. You can almost sense the heat of the nearest person or animal, and it leads you right to them and as their heartbeat increases so does the body heat and then." As she explained this to her husband, she unintentionally hypnotized Charles. "Are you listening to me?"

Charles just stood there not moving until Cassandra snapped her fingers in front of him and startled him awake. "What happened, I was listening to you and looking into your eyes when all of a sudden I felt paralyzed. I couldn't move at all, it felt like my brain had shut down."

"Please forgive me, it was my fault. My eyes can act as a sort of distraction and hypnotize my prey or victim, which stops them from screaming."

"That is truly amazing. Have you ever used your powers to kill anyone, I mean besides other than food?"

"Well, when I get angry I get a feeling like there is an animal or something powerful and dark inside me and it wants out. But unfortunately, there has been one time when

I let my anger take control of me and I have killed a few innocent as well as guilty people." Ashamed as she was, she told her husband what she had done. She didn't tell him what town she was in when she did it and she left out how many people really died. Or that she was the one who killed Edward.

<u>Chapter Two</u>

It had been about two years since Chloe had passed. As the time went by more servants disappeared and Charles became unwilling to hire new ones.

"I refuse to send sheep to the slaughter" as he told his wife, "Can't you drink the blood of animals? I have no problem purchasing actual sheep or cows or goats or whatever you choose. But I cannot, in good conscience, continue to hire new help just so you can kill them for food. I'm sorry if this seems cruel to you but the guilt is killing me and I won't do it anymore." Charles pleaded with his wife.

"No. I won't. I need human blood to fully sustain myself. Animal blood does not satisfy my hunger like human blood. Plus, animal blood is dirty and has a foul taste. I refuse to demean myself to appease your conscience."

Cassandra, who with all her heart loved her husband, was getting annoyed with his newly found conscience. She decided to put it to an end. Whenever she "fed", she always took the servants who were less obedient but this time she would take who was closer to her husband, and she knew exactly who it was. It was Jacob, the son of the carriage driver, who she murdered in Wills. She would take him, drain him of all his blood and leave his lifeless corpse somewhere where Charles would find it, and he would be forced to end the shortage of servants.

Cassandra began planning her revenge, little did she know of Charles's true feelings towards the boy. The consequences of her actions would change both of their lives forever.

Charles had always treated Jacob like a son. Partly because he felt responsible for his father's death, if Charles hadn't sent Edwards to check the church in Wills then he would still be alive. Edward would be the one raising Jacob, like it was supposed to be. The day Charles left Brooks with Cassandra, he swore to God that he would take care of Jacob and raise him as if he was his own son. Since that day, he had kept his word. After thinking of ways to break the news of his father, Charles finally told him.

Although it was a sugar coated version, it had seemed to help both Charles and Jacob deal with the tragedy..

Jacob seemed to find comfort in the fact that his father had died saving Charles. It gave him a sense of pride and honor to know his father was a hero before he was taken from him. Jacob gratefully accepted Charles's offer to help him with his education and took to Charles as a father figure very quickly. Charles on the other hand felt shame for having lied to Jacob but took some comfort in the fact that Jacob granted him forgiveness which gave him some peace of mind.

Cassandra had been watching Jacob ever since she first arrived with Charles. At first it was with guilt, knowing that she was the reason the boy was orphaned, but now it was with a sense of resentment. Charles had stopped hiring new servants and she took it extremely personally. She never took more than she needed to feed and sustain herself but her husband was now interfering with something he did not want to anger. So, she waited impatiently for her moment to make him regret crossing her.

She watched Jacob like a cat watching a mouse. She was waiting for the best time to take the one thing that mattered most to her husband. What fueled her rage was the fact that, she believed, Charles had replaced Chloe. His own flesh and blood, his baby girl, was replaced with an orphaned slave. She planned to make him pay dearly for his betrayal against their daughter.

Before Charles went to bed he had noticed his dear wife was acting quite strange. One thing was how flushed she appeared to be. The only other time she looked that way was in his dream before he met her. The second thing he noticed which also scared him the most was the look in her eyes. It was an intense animalistic look, as if something had possibly angered her. It was a look he had never seen before, and it scared him down to his bones. Something told him this night was going to be a bad one.

The fact that he didn't say goodnight to Cassandra didn't bother her but because he didn't say goodnight out of fear of her, saddened her. She knew what she was going to do would provoke an extreme reaction, but she had to do it even though she hated having her true love fear her. She had to make him see that their daughter, Chloe, could not and would not be replaced. She'd teach him this lesson and force him to understand.

Cassandra made her way upstairs to Jacob's room, she gently knocked on the door and called for the boy.

"Jacob, come to the door my dear boy." Cassandra used her most motherly voice to lure Jacob to the door

"Who… Who's there?" Jacob had awoken to the sound of knocking on his door. The voice, however, did not recognize.

"It's Cassandra, the lady of the house, Charles's wife. Please come to the door. I would like a word with you"

"Is Charles with you?"

"No, he sleeps as we speak." Cassandra was beginning to get impatient with the cowering boy. "Please come and speak with me for just a moment."

"Alright, I'm coming" Jacob slowly walked to the door to let her in. He thought that maybe since Charles was trying to be a father to him then maybe this woman would take to being a mother to him.

As soon as Jacob opened the door it was over. Cassandra pounced on him before he knew what was happening. She grabbed him by the throat and held him in the air. While he kicked and thrashed uselessly at her she glared at the boy with a deep hatred in her menacing eyes.

"How dare you try to take the place of my child in my husband's life. The nerve of you boy, for this you shall pay like your father did. WITH YOUR LIFE!!!" Cassandra bolted through the open window clutching Jacob's throat. As they hit the dampened grass she heard a loud snap. Looking back, she saw his shin bone protruding through the skin. The scent of fresh blood made her senses tingle, her mouth watered and her rage increasing as well as her burning hunger for revenge. Not only towards the boy but against her husband for trying to replace their daughter with a servant's son. His own flesh and blood with the blood of someone who she had for dinner over three years ago.

Even with a badly broken leg Jacob still put up a fight. When he tried to call for help Cassandra put her hand over his mouth. She kept her hand there, even when he bit her and almost made her bleed, she didn't remove her hand. Only when his frantic yells dulled into crying whispers did she loosen her hand on the boy's mouth. She had squeezed his face so hard he already had bruises forming on his cheek.

"There, there. Calm yourself boy. No matter how loud you scream or try to call for help, no one will come to your aid. Charles is sound asleep. And no one would dare come outside to check on someone screaming." Cassandra's eyes were glowing with hatred and Jacob could easily see it.

"I'm sorry. P…P…P…Please don't kill me. I will run away, I will leave and never return. I promise. Please ma'am. I'll do anything, anything you want." Jacob pleaded for his life willing to submit to anything opposed to dying. "I didn't mean to take the place of Miss Chloe. I loved her as if she was my own sister ma'am. Please spare me, I will leave and never speak of this night, I swear it."

"Swear and plead all you want, nothing will save you on this night. Your words are meaningless boy. Your life is the only thing I want, and I will have it."

Just as Cassandra went to bite Jacob, he was able to free a hand. With this small taste of freedom, he reached for a weapon. The only thing in reach was a rock not much bigger than his hand. With a loose grasp the boy swung the rock with the little strength he had left in his hand and hit his captor on the side of the head. Cassandra fell over onto her side, like a sack of potatoes. Jacob, with rock in hand slowly got up and crawled over to Cassandra, he saw the blood on both the rock and her head.

He moved closer to Cassandra and with his free hand, nudged her.

"Miss?" He called out in fear and pain. No response, He assumed he killed the creature with the rock.

With every ounce of strength, he was able to gather he lifted himself up and was leaning on a tree. With his leg broken he knew he couldn't get far fast enough. So, he used the trees to push off of. He had barely gotten over 5ft away from Cassandra when he heard a twig snap. Jacob shot around looking in the direction in which he left Cassandra lying. The only thing he saw was the bloody rock. The darkness of the night had begun to engulf him. He could barely see around him and they were so deep into the woods that he was unable to pick a direction to go to escape his doom.

Jacob's eyes began to fill up with tears, his body began to shake, and he was no longer able to use his good leg because of the fear which made it buckle. All of a sudden he heard it, the sound that told him he was about to die. The darkness seemed to part for her like a curtain as she spoke.

"Ha, Ha, Ha, Ha," Cassandra chuckled maniacally, "you think you can kill me with the rock? It'll take more than a single blow to the head to kill me. All you were able to do was anger me and for that you will not live long enough to regret." And with that said Cassandra leaped onto the boy slamming him onto the ground. Her nails, which had now become talon like, slashed at the boy's face, chest and arms as he tried to block her attacks. She then held his arms down and licked the blood off Jacob's face. The taste of blood set her senses tingling. Her eyes went from hazed to a bright blue. Two of her teeth grew at least an inch and her grip on Jacob's arms tightened incredibly.

Jacob watched Cassandra's transformation and was frozen with fear. The gaze in her eyes seemed to have a paralyzing effect on him even though he was scared to death. Cassandra released her grip on the boy's arms and he laid there. In his mind he was trying to scream and with all his might to move but she had somehow paralyzed him. He could only blink his tears away.

"Now, my dear boy you shall truly pay for trying to steal my husband's love from our daughter. Soon you will see your father again in the afterlife, so I am showing you mercy and ridding my husband of a false child. Goodbye."

Cassandra slowly turned Jacob's head, exposing his blood tainted neck. She ran her finger over his pulsing jugular and then leaned in smelling not only blood but all his fear. She took it in as if preparing to savor a gourmet dinner. With one flick of her finger, she slit the boy's throat. His blood began to pour out of his neck. As he gasped for any breath of air he could find, she sank her teeth into his neck and began to feast on his warm, young and sweet blood.

Jacob was doing the only thing her paralyzing gaze couldn't stop, he was crying. He could feel the pressure of her teeth pressing down on his neck. As she drank, every gulp made the hair on his body stand on end. As she drank her power over the boy began to fade. But as the power faded so did his strength. He could literally feel his life being drained from his body.

As Cassandra approached the last drop of Jacob's blood she stopped. She knew that with the last drop she would not only be taking his life, but it would mean that Charles would no longer have his replacement. She watched the boy's last moments, and she heard his last words in a whisper.

"I'm coming home Father. I'm coming home." And then he was gone.. Cassandra shed a tear because she knew her husband was going to be heartbroken as soon as he found out about the loss of Jacob.

Cassandra took the boy deeper into the woods, knowing that any of the wildlife who happened to discover the body would eat at his flesh. By doing this she would be covering up the gashes and marks that she had given the boy. She already knew her plan would work because in her peripheral vision she could see a lone wolf stalking her and her prey.

As Cassandra began her walk back to the house she calmed herself so that she would reverse the change that her feast had brought on. She had been extremely careful as to not get any of Jacobs blood on her and she had cleaned her face off on Jacobs shirt when she had finished her deed. As she got even closer to the house she began to force tears and began running to the door. She started screaming and calling for her husband.

"Charles… Charles. Come quick. Please come quick."

Racing down the stairs Charles was rubbing away the sleep that still lingered in his eyes.

"What is it? What's Wrong?"

"Jacob. He's gone. I went to speak with him in his room and he was gone. The window was broken and the ground outside had blood on it. I tried to look for him, but I heard growling so I came back as fast as I could to get you. Hurry my love. We must find him." Charles didn't even think to doubt his wife.

"Wait here. I will look for him myself. I wouldn't be able to forgive myself if anything happened to you." Charles took one of his rifles out of his gun case, loaded it, and took some extra shells in his pocket. He left his sobbing wife standing in the doorway and began his search for Jacob. He first went to the spot beneath the boy's window. Like Cassandra had said there was blood on the ground. Remembering that Cassandra said she tried looking for the boy, he saw footprints about her size. He followed them until he came to a rock about palm size with blood on it. He picked it up looking at the blood stain. Setting the rock aside he continued his search. Out of the corner of his eye Charles saw something move and began to move towards the object. He then realized it was a wolf and it was gnawing on something. About the size of a child. Charles shot off his rifle in the air and the wolf glared at him and faced him as if getting ready to attack him. Charles shot off another round and the wolf ran off with Jacobs blood dripping from its mouth. As Charles moved closer to the ravaged object he recognized what he was looking at, it was Jacob, lifeless and ravaged.

"My dear god. What has happened to this boy? Why would he want to run away, let alone jump out a window." As he said that he saw Jacob's broken leg. The bone protruding from his leg. The blood drenched clothes he was wearing left him in shock. The gashes, the claw marks and worst of all the look of absolute fear frozen on the boy's face. Charles broke down on the spot and began crying. He asked God and Jacob's father for forgiveness for failing to care for the boy. As Charles looked down he saw something in Jacob's hand and investigated it. It had been torn off of something, something like a shirt or blanket. It was very soft and stained red with his blood. The material seemed familiar to him, but he wasn't too grief stricken to figure out what it was from.

Charles placed the bloodied cloth in his pocket and picked up the boy's body. At first he struggled to lift Jacob, he was filled with determination, and he refused to leave the body for any other animals to feast on. He lifted him up with every ounce of strength he could find. He carried Jacob's body back to his estate and laid him down on the porch. He sent one of his servants to town to fetch the sheriff and the undertaker.

When the sheriff arrived, Charles hid the piece of cloth from them. Deep in the back of his mind, he had a sinister thought, could his beautiful wife have something to do with Jacob's Death. The coroner took Jacob's body away and Charles again began to cry. He had failed his friend, his brother. He failed to protect his daughter and now filled with hurt and regret he had let harm fall upon Jacob. He swore to himself that he would find out what happened and justice would be served for the boy.

Cassandra went to their room before her husband and had a chance to return. As she changed her clothes she noticed a piece of her dress had been torn. She assumed it got caught on a branch or something in the woods. She never thought that perhaps her revenge would be foiled by a dying servant boy.

<u>Chapter Three</u>

Charles had his suspicions about Jacob's death. He didn't want to believe that Cassandra would or could hurt the poor boy, especially after knowing all that he'd been through. She knew that Charles had sworn to protect and look after the boy ever since his father died. He had hoped that one day she would come to see Jacob as an adopted son. No one could ever replace their dear sweet baby Chloe, but he had come to see Jacob as a son. Plus, with him being older, Charles was more of a mentor to the boy, someone he could help become a respectable member of the community. But no longer. He had two holes in his heart now, one for his sweet baby girl and the other for Jacob.

Cassandra could see the heartache and turmoil building in her husband. She began to wonder if telling him the boy had run off and telling him where the body might have been was possibly a bad idea. She was normally much more careful and secretive about such things. Perhaps she acted a bit hastily, not fully thinking her plan through. After all, she did tear her dress and was unsure when or where it had happened. The piece that had been torn off was roughly the size of her palm and the tear was oddly shaped. She would have to venture out into the woods to see if she could find it. She knew that no one other than Charles was out that far that night and he hadn't mentioned anything to her.

It had been two days since Jacob was killed and a funeral had been planned for him. The day before he was to be laid to rest, next to his father, was when the body was to be examined by the undertaker. Instead, he came to see Charles. "Sir, I am at a loss for words, but the boy's body has been taken." The undertaker was filled with confusion and mortification.

"I beg your pardon, but did you say Jacobs body was taken? Why the hell would someone take the corpse of a young boy?" Charles was beginning to get very irate with the undertaker. "Did you notify the sheriff? What are you doing to find the body?"

"I'm very sorry about all this. I did speak to the sheriff, and he looked around the building but didn't find anything. He said he will continue to search but I came over immediately because I wanted to let you know about what was going on." The undertaker began walking away from the door to return to town.

"This is unbelievable. I don't understand who would do such a horrible and despicable thing. This poor boy cannot even rest in death." Charles was shouting at the undertaker as he walked away.

Cassandra could overhear the undertaker and Charles's conversation. Even she was shocked to hear that Jacob's body was taken. She feared that Charles would suspect her of taking the body, since she had admitted to discarding the bodies of the servants she fed on. She was beginning to regret sharing so much information with her husband. She began to feel paranoid and unsure of the outcome of what she had done. Granted she did get the revenge she desired, but now with the new development of the body disappearing his suspicion of her involvement was going to be high. The next time she fed it would have to be done somewhere distant from their home.

Charles had noticed that Cassandra was listening to him and the undertaker. He could see a look of curiosity on her face and it intrigued him. Why was she listening so

intensely? Was his suspicion about her harming Jacob true
or was he being mistrustful of his wife? Part of him wanted
to believe that she would never hurt him in such a manner
but deep down in the pit of his gut something was gnawing
at him. He knew of her, other self, and what she needed to
do to eat. He had to find a way to see if she knew anything
more than what she said the night Jacob was found. He
didn't want to falsely accuse her of something she may not
have done.

"Cassandra my dear, would you join me for dinner
please. I know that my food isn't enough for you, but I
would truly appreciate your company and presence. It has
been a trying and exhausting few days and the company of
my loving wife would surely help cheer me up. In all
honesty, I miss you my love." Charles smiled at his wife.
He decided that he would not jump to conclusions in regard
to Jacobs death and unfortunate disappearance.

"Really?" Cassandra was not expecting him to say
any of that and she seemed puzzled by her husband. "I miss
you too, my beloved. I feel as if we have become distant
with one another as of late and I crave your embrace and
affection." She smiled a genuine smile, "I would love to
join you for dinner."

Charles had an elegant meal prepared for them both. They sat down for dinner, they were smiling at one another, and it was a pleasant evening. They reminisced about the days after they first met and how quickly they fell in love. Both agreed that they would do everything all over again except maybe meet sooner as to avoid the circumstances that led to their meeting. He surprised her with a chocolate cake for dessert, he knew that she would absolutely love it, it was her favorite. He moved closer to her so he could serve her a piece, he cut off some with a fork and fed it to her. He could see in her eyes that she wholeheartedly enjoyed the cake and her husband feeding it to her.

Cassandra was thinking that the only thing she would do differently was not tell her husband her secret, though she would not admit that to him. She knew he would be hurt or offended, and she was enjoying this night far too much to want to do either. As she looked into his eyes, she could see the love that she so badly missed and in that moment she began to regret her actions against him. If only she could have seen Jacob as a son like her husband did, with that single thought, she felt conflicted. She began to feel as if she was betraying Chloe's memory but at the same time felt as if sharing that love was honoring her in some way. She shook off the feeling, realizing it was too late for such sympathies. She knew that she chose to keep her love solely for her daughter and she intended to stand strong with those feelings and her decision.

"My sweet love, I am sorry that it's been difficult as of late. I can see the heaviness that your grief bears on you, you are a great man with a big heart. Your love knows no bounds and has no limits." They were already sitting next to each other, but she moved closer and placed her hand on his face. "Come closer!" She whispered to him. As he leaned closer to her, she softly kissed his lips, and she heard his heart begin to beat faster. She kissed him again, this time pressing against his lips a little firmer and pulled him closer to herself.

Charles was surprised by the passionate kisses from his wife, he grabbed her hand and stood up. He led her to the bedroom, stopping every few steps to resume kissing one another. Once they got to the door Charles turned the knob slightly to just get it past the frame. He turned back to Cassandra, kissed her, scooped her up in his arms and carried her to the bed. He gently set her on the bed and laid down next to her. He wrapped her in his arms as they continued to kiss.

Each kiss, with more passion than the previous, got longer and deeper. They stood up for a moment. Charles had begun to unbutton the back of Cassandra's dress. As her dress slid off, she turned towards him, still in her slip. She unbuttoned his top three buttons, then in one movement she ripped his shirt open sending the remaining four buttons flying across the room. She then pushed him onto the bed, Charles was surprised by her strength. She climbed back onto the bed, straddling him, she leaned forward kissing him as his hands caressed her breasts.

With each second, their breathing got faster, and their heart rates increased. Charles tried to roll them over so that they would be laying on the bed facing each other. Cassandra resisted, and with a wild eyed look she leaned in kissing him on his neck. She could hear the blood flowing in the veins in his neck and something primal in her was triggered. Her kisses became more aggressive.

Charles tried to match her strength, but he could not. She had him pinned on the bed. "Cassandra, my love, I can barely move." He felt almost helpless, as he attempted to again roll them on their sides. She kissed him and as she backed away he could see that something was taking over in her eyes. A look that was pure animalistic, it frightened him. He tried to struggle but he could not move.

Cassandra felt the power in her grow, she knew Charles's strength could not match hers. With every breath he took, the rhythmic sound of his heart only increased her desire and lust towards him. She heard his request but didn't acknowledge his plea. However, a thought came across her mind, she could give him the gift of her power. With a single drop of her own blood, he could have a taste of the power that lies inside of her. This time when she kissed him she bit her lip ever so slightly, enough for one single drop to quickly pass from her lip to his tongue.

All of a sudden, Charles felt a surge of energy and strength. He had no clue where it came from, but he was able to finally move and now he was on top of Cassandra. His senses were on fire, their kisses felt more incredible than ever before. Even touching her skin, he felt like he was sliding his hand across silk. What stopped him in his tracks was how he could now hear her heart beating. He could see each and every vein pulsating with blood. And he wanted it, like that first sip of cold water on a scorching hot day in the sun. He needed it, like the crops needed the rain in the summer. Then he looked at Cassandra, she was smiling as if she accomplished something. "What did you do to me? I've never felt like this before. The power, the desire, the hunger. My senses are so heightened that even the slightest touch is so amazing. What is this?" Charles's voice had started to sound deeper to him, and his heart was beating faster than ever.

"It's a gift. A taste of the power that is in me and how my body reacts to you in this moment. Can you feel the power of our passion? Do you like the feeling of this power, my love?" Cassandra felt proud of herself. Perhaps he would want to share this feeling with her forever.

"It does feel amazing. I feel like I could fight a hundred men and win. I feel like I can out run the horses in the stable. But how? Why do I feel like I can do these things? Tell me please." Charles's emotions were all over the place and he was so confused.

"A single drop of my blood. I shared the power that's within me. I wanted you to see what could be possible for us both. I can make this feeling permanent. I can make us forever. We would never grow old and we would never die. At least not in the normal sense of the word." She had said to him. She could feel it in her bones that he was going to say yes.

"Your blood did this? What do you mean? How can you make this permanent and us forever? Cassandra, I am truly confused. How did you become like this?" He was now more worried than excited. How was any of this possible?

"Charles, I am much older than I have led you to believe. I'm not thirty years old, I'm actually two hundred and thirty years old. When I was twenty-five I was in Spain. I was visiting the countryside with my family, and I got separated from them. I came across an inn and paid the innkeeper for a room. I planned to find my family in the morning. I was awakened in the middle of the night by a dark figure standing at the end of my bed. I went to scream but the figure quickly covered my mouth. I could tell it was a man, but I couldn't see his face. I could feel his breath on my cheek, then he grabbed me by the neck. He whispered into my ear, "This will hurt, you will die but you will be reborn as something more, something of the night and you will live forever. Know this child, one day I may come for you, and you will be mine." He bit my neck, draining me of my blood but withheld the last few drops. He bit his wrist and fed me his blood. From that day I have been this creature that hides from the sunlight, out-living everyone I have ever loved."

Charles just sat there completely taken aback. Never in his wildest dream had he heard such a tale. He just sat there, staring at Cassandra, looking for the words but he could find none.

"That was how this happened, how I came to be this way. You asked how I can make what you are feeling permanent and make us forever. By doing the same that was done to me, except I would not abandon you to learn how to live this new life." Cassandra had told him what she had never told another single soul. "Do you have anything to say or ask Charles?"

"I'm sorry that this happened to you. I'm sure the years have been lonely, and you must have seen a great deal over your lifetime. Did you ever find your family?" Charles was saddened by her story, but he was also avoiding answering her question.

"Yes I did. Five months later I finally found my way home. I was lost in a sea of darkness and horror. I had to learn how to feed and what to do to keep myself alive. It was easier back then, to feed, to hide the remains. When I finally got to my home my parents just looked at me like they had seen a ghost. They said that I had not aged since they last saw me but that I seemed different. I couldn't tell them what happened because I knew they would never believe it. I made up a lie that I was held captive by French soldiers who sold me to a family to be a maid and nanny to their children. I told them I ran away in the night and managed to find my way home." She could see he was lost in the story, and his eyes showed the look of indecision. "What do you say husband, do you want to live forever?"

He sat a moment longer then got up and walked over to the nightstand to pour himself some whiskey. He downed a double shot and looked at his wife. "I can't answer you Cassandra. I love you dearly, but I cannot make that decision right now." He slowly looked up at his wife, and it was just in time to see her moving towards him with her unnatural speed.

She tried to be patient with him and gave him the decision on whether he wanted to join her in forever. His indecisiveness insulted her, so she was going to take the decision away from him. She would give him forever with her as the ultimate show of love. She hoped that afterwards he would see it that way as well. She launched herself at him knocking him onto the bed. She laughed in both a playful and sinister manner. He still had some of her strength lingering because he was able to hold her hands back. The more he struggled the faster his strength faded, until she was able to pin his hands back over his head. She pushed his head to the side, bared her long pointy fangs and was about to sink them into her husband's neck to give him eternity.

"NO!!!!! Stop this at once Cassandra. I don't want this…. This gift as you call it. It is no gift, it is a curse. To extend one's own life by taking others is not a way I choose to live." Charles used the last of the strength he had from Cassandra to yell this to his wife and these words cut straight to the bone.

Cassandra moved back and away from her husband. She just stood there, glaring at him with tears in her eyes. "So, Charles, you see me as a monster? You think I am cursed? How dare you, you cowardly fool. I offered you life beyond what you could possibly imagine. The things you would get to see and experience and you throw it back at me? What kind of man are you?" Cassandra, now filled with rage, began to move towards Charles. Her nails started growing and coming to a sharp point. She swiped at him, but missed, hitting the wall instead. The marks she left looked like a bear had just scratched the wall.

Charles stood there frozen in fear and disbelief. "How could you think it would be OK to force that on me? What kind of man am I? I am the man that loved you even after you told me your secrets. I am a man that believes all life is precious and one person should not pick whose life is worth less than another's. That's the kind of man I am. I told you I couldn't make that decision today, but you took it upon yourself to choose for me." His fear was being replaced by anger as he spoke to her. "I'm sorry Cassandra but I do not want this forced upon me. I will not become someone who kills innocent people for a meal."

"Who said anything about the innocent? You can feed off of those who have hurt people, those who have done evil things. You can be a hero in the shadows, doing justice when it cannot be done right. Not one single person would know your identity besides me, of course." She was trying to reason with him, trying to get him to see the benefits of her offer. "I will leave you to think about this. Either way I will wait for your answer. I will be in Chloe's room waiting." Cassandra stormed off and slammed the door once she was in the room. She hoped that her husband would willingly choose to be with her forever and that she wouldn't have to force this gift on him.

With a sigh of relief, Charles quickly closed the door to the room. He poured himself a glass of whiskey, this time filling the glass about 3 quarters of the way. With two big sips the glass was empty. He refilled the glass, but this time he drank slower. He looked at the scratches she left on the wall while sipping on his drink. As he inspected them, he realized they were very familiar. They looked just like the marks that were made on Edwards chest all those years ago.

As he stood there examining the scratches on the wall, he heard a faint tap at the window. He looked over quickly but was unable to see anything. He walked over, opened the window and leaned out to see if anyone was outside. He thought "there is no way anyone would be tapping on the window, it's at least 20 feet from the ground. Maybe a rock was thrown." He looked for a few moments before closing the window and returned to the bed. He knew he wouldn't be able to sleep but he tried anyway.

Cassandra was pacing in Chloe's room. She could not believe the audacity he had to call her a monster and say that she was cursed. The more she paced and thought about it, the angrier she got. It was to the point that she needed to leave the house. She opened the windows and jumped out, landing gently on the ground below. She sped

off into the woods to look for the torn piece of her dress.

She found the rock that Jacob had hit her with, she saw the

blood that stained it. She almost forgot that he was able to

draw blood from that hit. Brave boy. Foolish and futile to

try and defend himself but brave, nonetheless. She decided

she needed to feed so she rushed off to the edge of town.

She was able to find a man, drunk and stumbling out of the

saloon. She smiled at him and he followed her around to

the side of the saloon where she knocked him unconscious.

She picked him up and quickly ran off with him.

Once she had her fill, she snapped his neck and hid

his body in a nearby lake. She began walking around the

lake, looking up at the stars and enjoying the night breeze.

She sat under a tree, leaned up against it and closed her

eyes. She listened to the wind rushing across the grass and

over the leaves. She could hear the crickets singing in the

night and the bullfrogs croaking in the distance. She knew

her darling Chloe would have enjoyed this night.

Charles, like he guessed, couldn't fall asleep. He

couldn't stop thinking about the scratches on the wall and

that they were identical to the ones he had seen on Edwards

chest in Wills. He then remembered Cassandra telling him

about a time where, as she states, she let her anger take control of her and she killed some people both innocent and guilty. "Could she have been the one who massacred all those people in Wills? She never mentioned the name of the town, she purposely left that out when she told her story." Charles's mind was racing and he had a knot growing in the pit of his stomach. Had he married his best friend's murderer? Was she responsible for the deaths of both Edward and Jacob? Why did she choose him when she knew what she had done to Edward. More importantly than thinking of the past, what was he going to do and how was he going to prove it was her.

Cassandra awoke to the sound of a fish jumping in the water. As she looked at the lake she noticed something standing across from her on the other side of the water. It looked like a person, just standing there, watching her from across the water. As she started to make her way to the shadowy silhouette, it disappeared. Within a blink of an eye, it was gone. She continued to where she thought the figure was standing and she caught the hint of something familiar. She looked around, sniffing and hoping to catch a scent in the air. But she had no luck. She didn't even find any footprints to follow. She began to make her way home.

Charles should be asleep by now and the sun wasn't too far behind.

She arrived home. She saw something on the window that alarmed her, scratch marks on the outside of her and Charles's window. It looked as if something had climbed up the wall and was scratching the glass. She climbed back in through Chloe's window, closed it, locked it and drew the shades.

Charles heard the window close and lock. He knew she was now back home and would be sleeping for a while, especially with the sun coming up soon. He would take that time to investigate his home and see if he could find anything to prove that Cassandra was in fact the monster of the Wills massacre. He would begin the process of finding justice for his friend and his son. No matter the cost.

As Charles stood at the window waiting for the sun to come up, he noticed something in the distance. A person standing next to a tree, a person who seemed very familiar to him. Then in an instant it was gone, but to him it wasn't an it. If he was right, it was someone very dear to him but how could it be? How could Jacob be standing next to a tree when Charles saw his corpse being mauled by a wolf?

Chapter Four

"What could have done such a thing to this boy?

"From what the master of the house said, it was a wolf. The wife found the boy when she went to speak to him. The window was shattered like someone had jumped out of it, she followed the footsteps she discovered outside which led to the boy."

"But that doesn't make a bit of sense. Why would someone jump out of a window only to be killed by a wolf. Even if the boy was trying to run away, could a single wolf take him down and kill him in such a way?"

"I agree, some foul play is definitely happening here. I don't believe the master of the house had anything to do with his death. However, I think the wife appears to have a dark side to her. Something in her eyes chills my soul."

"Sir, did you see that? His h…hand, it… it moved."

"Nonsense, you should know by now that the muscles of the body do that after it dies. What kind of undertaker do you plan on being, one afraid of a corpse or one with some stones?"

"Stones sir, I will be one with some stones. I was just momentarily caught off guard, it won't happen again."

"Maybe we should call it a night. It has been a long and trying day. Go home. We will meet back here in the morning and prepare the body and casket for burial."

"Yes sir, Good night."

There was a long silence that was disturbed by the sound of a loud gasp.

"Hello? Is anyone there? What is going on?" There was a loud thud as Jacob rolled off the undertakers table and hit the floor. He tried to push himself up, but he only cried out loud from the excruciating pain that was tearing through his body. He laid there wondering how he was still alive. After hearing what the undertaker and his associate said, he was baffled.

He tried to get up again, but this time he noticed something different. The pain was decreasing and he was able to get to a sitting position. Within moments, the pain was gone and he was making his way to his feet. As he stood up, he stumbled with that first step and caught himself on the very table that he fell off. Then he remembered what happened. "It was no wolf attack, SHE did this to me." He yelled out. He remembered she chased him down like a wild animal and she attacked him. But how was he alive? He knew that he had struck what should have been a devastating blow to her head with a rock. When he hit her it was hard enough that her blood had spilled onto his face and chest, especially when she bit his neck he felt the blood dripping on his wounds.

"Could her blood have done this? Did she infect me with whatever curse that lived in her veins?" He wondered, as he began walking to the door of the undertaker's office. He could feel his strength increasing and as he looked down he could see the wounds on his chest were closing. "What in God's name is happening to me? How is this even possible?" He started to wonder what else he was able to do? Cassandra was able to move at unnatural speeds, her strength was more than he would have guessed and she could clearly see in the dark of night.

As he opened the door, he felt the rush of the night air and his senses were on fire. He could hear people laughing in the saloon down the street, he could hear the sound of the crickets jumping and there was an aroma in the air that stirred something in him that he never felt. He started to run and in the blink of an eye he was standing on the steps of the saloon. Jacob decided not to go in since he didn't know who was all aware that he had died and was supposed to be on the undertakers table. He ran back home, stopped near a big tree and he gazed upon the place where he had grown up. The place that he and his father called home. The place where the only people he ever knew as family had lived and where he met the monster who took it all away.

He made his way to the side of the house, it was still night out, but he was careful and made sure that he wasn't seen. He went around back to check if the window to his room had been repaired yet and unfortunately it was fixed. He noticed that the window was slightly open, he could tell because he was able to hear the faint sound of the wind rushing through the small opening. He knew he had to get in without alarming Charles or Cassandra, he grabbed one of the bricks and he felt his nail grow and dig into it. He smiled as he grabbed another one and began pulling himself up to his window. He could not believe the strength he possessed and how easily he was pulling himself up. Once he reached the window, he gently began to lift it open and slid inside.

It seemed so strange to Jacob that he had to sneak into what was once his home. He went to his closet, grabbed some clothes, shoes and some money he had saved for the day he decided to move. It was Charles's idea that he start saving money, he said maybe one day you'll want to travel and see the world or even live in a different part of it. He was grateful for all that he had learned from Charles, he knew that because of him he would be able to succeed in life and survive whatever lies ahead of him. Although, there were some new trials that not even Charles could prepare him for, such as coming back from the dead and dealing with this curse that was forced on him.

Now that Jacob had what he needed, he looked at the door that led to the hallway. He could sneak down, find Cassandra and kill her before she even knew what was happening. He stood there contemplating his next steps. If it weren't for Charles, he would exact his revenge on that horrid monster. But he couldn't do that to Charles, not after everything he had done for him and all the kindness he had been shown over the years. Jacob opened the window, looked back at the door and then proceeded to jump out to the ground. He landed softly and without making a single sound. He noticed that the sun would be coming up soon and he wanted to be on his way before anyone knew he had been there or that he had walked out of the undertaker's office on his own. As he made his way to the trees, he stopped and faced the house as if to say good-bye. At that very moment he saw Charles walk up to the window and just stand there looking out at the sky. Then Charles looked in his direction and Jacob ran as fast as he could so he wouldn't be seen. But was it too late, it seemed like Charles looked directly at him.

Over the past few days, Charles had this strange feeling that he was being watched. Every time he passed a window he had the eerie notion that eyes were on him, but he never saw anyone when he would stop and look. A few times, at night, he noticed a shadow near one of the trees, but when he moved closer to the window the shadow was gone. At one point, a couple nights ago, he could have sworn he saw Jacob near the same tree. He knew it had to be his eyes playing tricks on him because Jacob was dead. He had seen the poor boy's body with his own eyes and after the mauling that wolf had done, there was no way he could have survived.

He wished that it wasn't just his imagination playing tricks on his eyes. Not only did he miss Jacob, but he would ask him about what happened that night in the woods. Why did it look like he jumped out of the window or was it something far worse? Were his suspicions that it was his beloved wife, true? Why would she do such a horrific thing to someone she knew meant so much to him? Or were his suspicions and accusations false and Jacob was unhappy with them? So many questions ran through his mind and with no answers he was tormented by the "What ifs".

Charles was sitting in his study when he had an idea, he would set a trap. He thought that if he hid in a tree, where his mind kept placing Jacob, he could possibly catch whomever was out there. At the very least, if he found nothing, his mind would be at peace knowing that Jacob was truly gone and no one was outside watching him. Since it was always at night when he saw him, Charles would wait till morning to make a sitting spot in the tree. He knew Cassandra would be fast asleep so she wouldn't be suspicious about his activities. He would take a quick nap to pass some time and then go to town to pick up supplies.

While Charles slept he had a vivid and frightening dream that Cassandra was chasing him throughout their home. He made it to the basement and was able to lock the door from the inside. He stood there, staring in absolute fear, as she was pounding on the door and screaming for him to open it. He could hear the sounds of her nails clawing at the wood of the door. He could see splinters of wood blowing under the door while she was frantically trying to get to him. He ran down the basement stairs and fell over something in the dark. He was able to light a nearby lantern and gasped in horror as he looked around the room. There were bodies laying all over the floor, they lay there with fear frozen on their faces and their clothes were drenched in blood. He looked down at his feet to see what he had tripped over, and it was Jacob's corpse. His mouth contorted with his jaw fully extended, the broken bone in his leg was protruding through the skin soaking his pants in blood. Large, deep claw marks ravaged his chest, and his neck had a large chunk of skin missing. The wound on his neck was so extensive that you could see the muscles torn and a thick vein oozing with coagulated blood. As he moved the lantern closer to Jacob's body he could see hundreds of maggots feasting on what was once someone very dear to him. Charles turned around to vomit but was shocked to see the basement door burst open with shards of wood flying everywhere around him. There she stood, at the top of the stairs, with an evil smile on her face as she lunged down the steps. She moved so fast it seemed as if she was flying down into the basement. Her hands hit his chest and he flew across the room. With sharp stabbing pain that he felt all over his body, he bounced off of the cement wall. As he was about to hit the floor, he woke up on the floor of his study. It seemed he fell off the sofa in his study and hit the floor at the same time he was going to hit the floor of the basement.

Charles sat there for a moment, before he got up, gathering himself and attempting to shake off the haze of the nightmare he just had. He couldn't believe how real it felt, his body was even feeling sore from crashing into the basement wall. He got up, poured himself a shot of whiskey and made his way to the barn to ready his horse. He only planned on getting a few things to set up his sitting post, so he left by himself and went into town. When he arrived, he noticed some of the people in the town staring at him and whispering to each other. He could only assume it was about Jacob's body disappearing. He made his way to the supply store.

"Good morning sir, how can I help you today?" The shop owner knew Charles and his family. "Got a new shipment of rifles and handguns today, would you like to see them?"

It was like he was reading his mind, thought Charles. "Actually, yes I would and I need other items. I'll need a two foot barrel lid, four 3 inch nails and some rope."

"That's a specific and short list but I'll get right on it. The rifles and pistols are hanging up there on the wall. Feel free to handle them and see what suits you." The shop owner knew Charles was trustworthy, so he left him to inspect the guns.

Charles had several rifles already at home plus he was more interested in the handgun. One in particular, it looked silver plated and felt great when he held it. "Is this pistol silver plated?"

"Yes sir, it sure is. Quite the piece that one. I've never seen one like it, truly one of a kind. I've been tempted to keep it for myself but if you're interested I'll give ya a great deal on it. How about an even twenty for the gun and the supplies?"

Charles had never worn a gun on his side, but with what had been going on lately it seemed like a good idea. "I'm going to need a holster and some ammo please."

"I had a feeling you were going to say that, have it for ya shortly. And it's on the house. Consider it a package deal for the gun purchase."

"Very much appreciated." Charles smiled at the shop owner as he handed him the money for his purchase.

"It's been my pleasure helping you today sir. I look forward to seeing you on the next one."

Charles threaded his belt through the holster's belt loops and then slid it around his waist. He placed the gun into the holster, after loading it and headed outside to his horse. Luckily the items he purchased fit in his satchel, he loaded them up and began his trip home. With every gallop from the horse, he felt the gun bouncing at his side. He was hoping he wouldn't need it, but something drew him to it and now he needed to prepare to use it.

Once he arrived home, he headed over to the tree where he often saw the shadowy figure. While on his horse he threw one end of the rope over a large branch and tied the ends together. He stood up on the horse's back and using the nails and a hammer he placed the barrel lid on the large sturdy branch. He placed the nails two next to each other and about an inch apart. The makeshift seat felt solid and would surely be enough to keep him sitting comfortably in the tree for the night. He would use the rope to climb up to his sitting spot, then pull it up to use a lasso and capture his mystery figure.

He headed back to the house for something to eat and to figure out how to keep Cassandra from being alarmed that he wasn't home. As he ate, he wrote a note for Cassandra that he would go to the next town over to oversee a gift he was having made for her. Luckily he had already been planning something for her. It was a custom chair that was going to be made with the finest fabrics and would be the softest chair so she could sit comfortably in front of the fireplace. It was all working out perfectly, in the back of his mind he thought it was working out a bit too perfectly and that made him very nervous.

After he finished eating, he had two of his staff take
two horses and the wagon to the next town over. He gave
them instructions to stay the night at one of the inns and
bring the chair back with them. He gave them money for
food and for the room. Once they were on their way, he
began to make his way out to the tree where he set up his
spot. As he walked over to the tree, he loaded up the gun he
had purchased earlier. It was a six shooter and he spun the
barrel after making sure it was all set and then he put it in
the holster. Using the rope, he pulled himself up into the
tree and made himself as comfortable as he could get. He
made sure he was surrounded by the branches of the tree, to
keep himself hidden from both Cassandra and whatever it
was that he had hoped to catch. He pulled the rope up and
looped it around his arm. With one end he set up the lasso
part so he could trap his shadowy stalker, if there actually
was one.

A few hours after the sun went down Charles was
starting to get tired, he began to wonder if he was crazy and
possibly just wasting his time. He noticed the lights in the
house being turned on and saw Cassandra walk past a
couple of the windows. He was thinking about how
ridiculous it was that he was sitting in a tree because he
thought the ghost of his friend's dead son was watching

him. He was about to give up when he heard a twig snap. He unlooped some of the rope making sure he had enough give to be able to drop it down and hopefully around a person, not some wild animal.

He waited as he heard some footsteps making their way towards the tree. He could feel his heart beating like a hammer hitting a nail. Then he heard a sigh and saw something step under the branch he was sitting on. It was like whatever it was, knew he was there and wanted to be caught. As insane as that seemed to him, he dropped the loop of the lasso down and around the figure. It was too easy, yet he jumped down from the tree with the rope on the other side of the branch. As he went down to the ground, the rope on the figure tightened. He pulled the gun out of its holster at the same time his feet hit the ground. He aimed it at the shadow stalker and he couldn't believe what he was seeing.

"How are you still alive? I saw your body that night, it was lifeless and ravaged. Answer me Jacob or God help me I will shoot you." Charles was angry, confused and relieved all at the same time.

"I don't think your bullets will do very much to me in my current state, but I am curious to see if I'm wrong."

Jacob smiled and chuckled. "How am I alive? Well, I think we have your wife to thank for that. I woke up in the undertaker's office on a table, and I was just as confused then as you are now."

"Cassandra? She did this to you? I had a terrible feeling that she was responsible, but I didn't want to believe it. I…. I am so sorry my boy. I had hoped she wasn't capable of such a horrific act." Charles began to feel the tears welling up behind his eyes. He took a breath to try and compose himself as he looked at Jacob.

"Unfortunately, Charles, she is far more capable than you think. She wanted revenge against you for treating me like a son after Miss Chloe passed. She said you betrayed your daughter by taking to me. She threw me out the window of my room and hunted me down like a starved lion. She drained my blood but in the process she bled into my wounds." Jacob felt his anger rise for a moment but knew it wasn't Charles he wanted to unleash the rage on.

Charles stood there with an angry stare. He could tell Jacob was aware of the anger inside him and he could see the anger inside his friend as well. "She bled into your wounds? How? She knows her blood contains the power to make others like her, I didn't think she could be so careless."

"When she attacked me out here, I hit her in the head with a rock. I thought she was dead at first, but she came to and intended on finishing her work. When she caught me and made me her dinner, she was still bleeding. That's when she bled into my wounds and how I became cursed." Jacob had a look of sadness while telling Charles about his murder. The look changed from sadness into suspicion. "Wait, how did you know that her blood contained her power? Did you know she was going to come after me?"

"How can you think that of me? If I had known her intentions towards you, I would have sent you far away. So far that her hands or teeth couldn't touch you. I know because after your death, which she had me believe was done by a wolf, she gave me a taste of her power. When she kissed me, she slipped a drop of blood into my mouth, that single drop gave me a brief taste of her power. The strength, heightened senses and an unbearable urge to feed on blood." Charles hadn't realized that he was still pointing his gun at his lassoed friend.

Jacob stretched his arms against the rope as Charles put his pistol away, with one big stretch it snapped. Charles stood there in shock and amusement. "I'm still getting used to this strength, I suppose not all of this curse is terrible, but I would not wish it upon anyone. I do have to ask, what was the answer you gave her? Are you going to join her or deny her?"

"I won't lie to you Jacob, there are parts of what she was offering that are truly tempting. But the more I think about it, the more I realize she may be the monster who killed your father and an entire town. And that… that is more than enough to make me deny her and crave revenge of my own. She took my family away from me. She took you, your father and I have no doubts that she is the reason Chloe died." He dropped the rope since Jacob already freed himself and he braced himself against the tree. The anger washing over him was stronger than anything he had ever felt.

"I hate to tell you this, especially because I can feel your anger, but you are correct. She is the monster you fear she is. She admitted it to me as she hunted and fed on me. I am sorry to confirm your fears, but you need to know what and who you're living with." Jacob could tell that his words cut Charles deep and straight to his heart. He watched a single tear roll down his friend's face.

"I don't want to believe you Jacob, but I do. As much as it breaks my heart, I truly do believe you and I am so sorry that I brought this nightmarish monster into our life and that she took yours. I am so very deeply sorry, but I am going to need your help. I want vengeance. For your father, for you and for my sweet baby Chloe." Charles began to turn around, and he placed his hand on the pistol on his hip. He was about to step towards the house when Jacob placed a hand on his shoulder.

"Not yet. Her time will come and yes I will help you, but we can't go running inside that house right now. If we do, we are both dead the moment we step inside, and we would have died for nothing. We have to come up with a plan but first we need more information. We have no idea what can kill her or even hurt her. As much as I really hate to say this, we need to test out theories, and I may be our only way of figuring this out." Jacob was well aware of what that could mean for him, but they had to be sure the plan was solid and permanent.

"I won't put your life at risk any more than I have already." Charles couldn't bear the idea of hurting Jacob in order to exact revenge on his wife.

"Don't be stupid Charles. We don't have any other choice or ways to see what can hurt her. I already know that the sun hurts like a son of a bitch, but I can heal from it, meaning so can she. I've only spent a moment in the light to see how long I can stand the pain. However, I do believe that if we don't get to shade and stay in the sun it may kill us, her. Beyond the sun, I don't know what else will help us." Jacob was serious about finding any way of hurting her and he didn't care if it meant hurting himself in the process.

"This gun I purchased is silver plated. I've never seen anything like it and the shop owner said it was one of a kind. Maybe that has some significance or maybe I'm just grasping at straws. I do know Cassandra isn't a fan of churches, but she did massacre everyone in that church, so I don't know if that has any weight to it." Charles was scared and sad at the same time. Deep down he loved Cassandra so much but with his suspicions confirmed he wasn't so sure anymore.

"As much as I don't want to be shot, perhaps tomorrow we can test that idea out. Since I can work at night, I can do some research and see if I can find any books or people who have dealt with someone like Cassandra. Surely she is not the first or only creature like her that exists, which honestly is a terrifying thought." Jacob was staring at the house as he spoke to Charles. He wanted to end her himself, but he knew that Charles wouldn't allow him to do so.

"Have you discovered any other abilities besides your strength? I remember when Cassandra gave me that taste of her powers. My senses were on fire, I could hear the sound of a heart beat through the walls, I could smell the night air, and the light of the stars were like millions of tiny suns lighting up the sky. Something else I remember, when she first revealed her true self to me, her eyes were able to put me in a trance or hypnotize me. Her nails grew into these animal-like claws too, she left quite the mark on our wall." Charles felt an ice cold chill run down his spine as he spoke of Cassandra.

"I am far too familiar with her claws and her bite. She never put me in a trance, I believe she wanted me to feel every moment, and she enjoyed the taste of my fear.

My senses are definitely stronger, I knew you were sitting in that tree as I approached it. I could hear your heartbeat, and I caught your scent about two miles back. I am able to move at faster than normal speeds, something that Cassandra can easily do as well." Jacob could see the look of shock and surprise on Charles's face.

"It's certainly impressive, the things you can now do, but the cost one must pay to obtain them is not. I can honestly say that I now have the answer to Cassandra's offer, no. I'm sure if we both possessed her powers we could easily eliminate her but I refuse to become like her. I know you had no choice and I mean no offense to you, but she is a monster. And you, Jacob, are not. We will defeat her, I will do whatever it takes to ensure it." Charles, filled with determination, knew he had to have a backup plan just in case they were unable to kill her. He would not let her harm another person ever again.

Neither of them realized that they had been out by that tree for so long that the sky was beginning to lighten. Charles knew that Jacob had to leave and seek shelter before the sun came up. He told him of an old house that was about a mile north of the main house. It belonged to him and it was very rarely ever used. Charles used to go there as a child to hide from his parents, so Jacob would be well hidden from both the sun and Cassandra. He told Jacob they would rest for the day and meet tomorrow. Charles would come up there around noon and they could begin their plans to eliminate Cassandra from their lives.

Charles could see his two servants heading back to the main barn with the chair secured to the wagon. He made his way to the barn to meet them and help get the chair inside the house. Once it was safely inside and set up next to the fireplace he made his way to his study to take a quick nap. He knew the days ahead of him would be both mentally, physically, and emotionally exhausting but in the end it would be worth it. It would be worth whatever sacrifices he had to make, even if it meant himself. Riding the world of the monster that Cassandra was would be worth any price.

<u>Chapter Five</u>

As Charles expected, Cassandra loved the new chair. She had spent the last few days sitting in it by the fire and writing in her journal. Charles was very curious as to what she wrote about. What could a two-hundred-year-old vampire have to journal about and what secrets did she stored away in there? He wondered if she had known any others like her and if she somehow still kept in contact with them. On the darker side, he thought about if she had made any enemies over the years. Surely someone as old as she was, especially with how vengeful she was, had made a few enemies along the way. He wanted to see what she was hiding in that journal and the only way it would be possible was to either steal it or see if she would allow him to read it.

"Cassandra my love," he shuddered using those words, "what do you write about in that journal of yours?" Charles would try the path of least resistance before any attempts to steal it.

"Well, my beloved, I have been writing or journaling for years. My parents insisted on it after I came back home, after being made into what I am now. They thought that if I wrote down my horrible nightmares, it would help them go away. Unfortunately, they didn't go away. When my parents read my journal, they learned about what happened and what I had become, they abandoned me. They left me while I slept, leaving only a note calling me an abomination and curse on our family and this world." She looked down with tears rolling down her face.

Charles pitied her for a brief moment, if she hadn't been the cruel, lying and murderous monster he knew her as, he would have felt something other than hate for her. Nevertheless, he knew he had a part to play in order to stop her, so he walked over to her and hugged her to comfort her. "I'm sorry you had to experience that, no one should ever have to know the pain of losing their family and living life so alone." He was drawing from his own pain with those words, and it was a pain that she caused him.

"Thank you my love, I appreciate your kind words. I am so grateful to have you in my life, I was so lonely and filled with rage for so long. Then the day we met, I felt something inside me change. My rage was replaced with purpose, belonging and that was all thanks to you." She knew her rage was in part the reason she found him and despite the fact that she had killed Jacob and Edward, she did love her husband.

"I was wondering if you would allow me to read your journals, I am so curious of the life you have led and all the wonders you must have seen. You have told me of the night that you became as you are, which has not sent me running, so you have nothing to fear." He could feel his heart beating slowly increasing, he knew he had to try and keep himself calm so she wouldn't suspect anything.

"I'd rather you not read them, husband. There are some dark and horrible things in these journals, and I do not wish to change how you see me. My past is a horrible bloodied nightmare and the things I had done before meeting you are truly ghastly." Cassandra was able to hear his heartbeat increase and immediately calm itself. It seemed as if he knew to calm himself but why? Was it fear or excitement about possibly reading her journals? It seemed very strange to her, but she dismissed the thought.

He was disappointed that she was not willingly going to allow him to read her journals, which meant he was going to have to come up with a plan to steal them and read them. "It's ok my dear, I understand your hesitation. I will give you your privacy as you continue your writing. Should I add another log to the fire, it feels a bit drafty in here." He walked over and grabbed a log and placed it on top of the already burning logs.

"Charles, have you given any thought to my offer? I know the other night became a bit intense, but it was only because my love for you is so strong and my passion got the best of me. I admit I did get carried away but it's only because one day you will be old and I will have to watch you die. I cannot bear the thought of living this life without you." Cassandra stared at her husband as he added the log to the fire and while he stood there. He stoically stood in place, arm on the mantle of the fireplace and staring at the fire.

As Charles stood there he watched the flames dance around the fireplace. They reminded him of his Chloe when she would jump around in the winter snow, playing so innocently and full of life. He turned and looked at Cassandra, thinking he could either live forever with her or one day die and be reunited with his sweet baby Chloe. He would see her again, he would see his parents again, he would see Edward once more and apologize for failing him when Jacob needed him the most. "I have given it great thought since you asked and as much as you will not like my answer, I must respectfully decline your offer. I do not wish to be immortal. One day, when I am that old man you speak of, I will die and I will be reunited with our sweet Chloe. I know it is not the answer you want but it is the only I can live with."

Cassandra glared at Charles. "I see that you have truly given this much thought and you are right, it is not the answer I wished for. You'd selfishly choose death over me? You believe that after you die you will be reunited with our child, well dear husband, you are heartbreakingly wrong. When you die your body will be buried and there will be nothing for you. There is no afterlife waiting for you nor is there a heaven or hell. There is only the here and now, so you'd rather just disappear into nothing. Perhaps you need some more time to think about your decision."

"So, you do not believe in heaven or hell, God and the devil? After all you have seen in your very long life, you doubt there is more than just what we are now? I suppose that explains part of the reason why you never wanted to attend church or maybe you are afraid. Afraid that one day, if you die, after the long life you have had you believe God won't let you into heaven. As you said your past is horrible and bloody, so it would seem that a fear of what may come next is reasonable." Charles just looked at Cassandra, he knew what he believed in and his convictions were rock solid. He wasn't sure if what Cassandra was, was the work of the devil, but he knew her heart was without a doubt touched by him.

"You dare suggest that I, an immortal being who can do things you can only dream of, is afraid of something that has no power over me. You are either incredibly brave or completely naive. To think your beliefs, have more ground and strength than the experience of someone older than anything you will ever know." Cassandra was conflicted. She didn't know whether to laugh at her husband or be angry with him. "Your words are laughable and irritating at the same time. I think you should head to your study, pour yourself a drink and think on your words to me."

Charles felt an anger and strength rising from his gut. "You think I should fear you and cower at your feet, just because you are something that has lived through the ages and has never been challenged? Wife, you do not know me very well, I do not back down from anyone or anything. Not only because of my beliefs but because that is the man I am. So no, I will not run away like a dog with my tail between my legs just because you tell me too. You may be this long lived being with incredible power, but I DO NOT FEAR YOU." Charles spoke with an impassioned and penetrating tone that left Cassandra in a state of shock.

Cassandra was completely astonished by her husband's words. "Perhaps it is I who should leave the room. No one in all my years has ever spoken to me in that manner or with such audacity. I am impressed husband. And with that being said" Cassandra stood up from the chair her husband had given her. "I will wish you a goodnight and leave you to your thoughts." She defeatedly walked away from Charles and made her way to her room. Never in her life had anyone made her feel so powerless, it was a new feeling, and she did not like it.

Charles took a breath of relief and sat down in Cassandra's chair. It felt like a small victory, one which he knew would not last since his wife was not familiar with defeat. She may have accepted it this time, but he knew that she may not allow it to happen a second time. He had never used that tone or spoke to anyone in that manner ever in his life. But it felt good, it felt right, like he was given a new sense of confidence for standing up for himself and his beliefs. He would enjoy this moment because in the very near future a battle for his life would begin.

Charles woke up in his study to see the sun was beginning to peek over the clouds. He knew that it meant that he had a busy day awaiting him. Once he was sure Cassandra was sleeping he would leave to meet up with Jacob. He checked his pistol, strapped it to his belt and made his way to his horse. He headed to the back property that he told Jacob about, he took a slightly longer path there to ensure he wasn't followed. When he arrived, he noticed there were new shutters on the windows. Clearly Jacob had been busy making sure the sunlight was kept out and that no one could see inside. Charles dismounted from the horse, tied the reins near the water trough that was in front of the house and he knocked on the door.

"Charles, you don't have to knock on the door, it is your property after all, and it may seem strange if someone sees you knocking on the door of a house that is supposed to be empty." Jacob was snickering as he called out to Charles.

"I suppose you're right, but it is just polite to do so either way. How have you been, my friend? I see you added some new shutters to keep the light away."

"Yes but more so for privacy. As far as the town is concerned, technically, I am supposed to be dead. Unless, and this is just an idea, if someone comes by I can say I am a cousin to my father Edward. This would be an easy explanation for quick matters." Jacob had already been using an alias when he was seen in town, though not many people knew him prior to his death. That made some things easier and created far less confusion.

"That's a good idea, however, I would still keep my distance from the main house. I assume that Cassandra would be able to recognize your scent and we definitely do not need that kind of trouble. At least not yet." Charles knew eventually they would have to face her, but Jacob was the ace up his sleeve, and he intended on keeping that secret for as long as possible.

"Well let's get to it. I know sunlight hurts us pretty bad, I'm sure it can probably kill us if we do not find shelter immediately. I've been speaking to some of the more superstitious locals and heard that garlic, silver and wooden stakes through the heart seem to hurt or kill vampires.

That's what we're called apparently, vampires." Jacob noticed the lack of surprise on Charles's face when he mentioned the name vampire. "I see you have heard that before, haven't you?"

"Cassandra called herself a vampire. I wasn't sure if it was just something she made up or not, but it seems to be true according to the information you have learned. I'm not sure how we test any of those methods you mentioned though, I mean the wooden stake through the heart sounds like a solid one. I suppose if you hold my gun and there is a reaction that's proof enough, same with the garlic. But honestly, I'm not entirely comfortable testing these methods on you. You have endured enough pain and subjecting you to more just doesn't feel right." Charles looked down in shame because he knew they had no other choice but to test out these methods on Jacob.

"I had a feeling you were going to say that, as much as I do appreciate the sentiment, I have prepared something to help ease your concerns. Please don't be angry with me but as you said I have been very busy. While I was searching for answers and ways to end Cassandra, I came across another like us. Another vampire." Jacob looked at

Charles waiting to see a reaction, whether it be anger, disgust or relief.

"You found another vampire? How many vampires are out there? And how are we supposed to torture someone who has done us no harm? I don't know about this plan Jacob." Charles was conflicted about the fact that his friend was holding another vampire hostage and planned to use him so they could figure out how to kill Cassandra.

"True, he did not do us any harm, but he volunteered. He said he was turned against his will and he doesn't want to live a life where he is a murderous monster. I know this sounds difficult to believe and I almost didn't believe it myself but he begged me to take him. He begged me to let him help us and then to promise to end his existence." Jacob let a bit of excitement show for a moment but was confused by the look Charles was giving him.

"He wants to die? I'm not saying I don't believe you Jacob, but it almost seems too good to be true. At a time when we can leave nothing to chance, we must be sure that he is not working with Cassandra. So, when he agrees, in front of us both, he cannot leave this house. Not until we carry his corpse out of here." Charles had a look of determination and purpose. He knew, as long as this man was serious, this would be their best chance to make a solid plan to finish Cassandra permanently.

"I completely understand and I agree with you one hundred percent. Let's go speak to him, he's resting in the back room. His name is Samuel, he's originally from Georgia. He was turned about thirty years ago, and he claims he doesn't know who his maker is." Jacob began walking with Charles to the room where Samual was resting.

Jacob knocked on the door. "Samuel, it's Jacob and I brought my friend that I told you about."

Samuel opened the door. "Please come in."

As they walked into the room, Charles noticed that Samuel was about five foot ten inches tall, easily weighed about two hundred pounds, dark brown hair and looked like he was in his early twenties. "Hello Samuel, I'm Charles, it's nice to meet you. From what Jacob tells me, you are a vampire and you want to help us?"

"As crazy as I'm sure it may sound, yes I do want to help but I do want something in exchange. Once you figure out what hurts us, I want you to test it out fully, I wish to die. I know how morbid this may sound but I simply cannot live with being this cursed monster. I want to finally rest and be at peace." Samuel looked at Jacob and Charles, eyes full of remorse and sadness.

After a brief moment of silence between the three men, Charles spoke. "Samuel, if that is what you need, then we will agree to your terms. I promise afterwards we will give you a proper burial, one that is respectful and dignified."

"Thank you, but please burn my body first. If you wish to bury the ashes afterwards then that is up to you, but it is not necessary. Fire is the most absolute way to make sure everything stays dead." Samuel had a stone cold serious look on his face. He did not want to leave anything to chance.

"We will respect your wishes. I personally wish to thank you, this whole thing has become quite personal and you sir are a true hero in my book. The toll it has taken on myself is beyond words and I'm not sure how much longer we can continue the charade of living with this monstrous woman. With that being said, thank you and if there is anything you need, please do not hesitate to ask." Charles was truly grateful for Samuel's sacrifice.

Jacob also spoke to Samuel. "See, I told you he was a good man, he only seeks redemption for his family he has lost. This woman made me what I am now but I refuse to allow her actions dictate how I will become. If my life is what it takes to end hers, I will proudly make that sacrifice. Thanks to you, we will have a fighting chance to accomplish this."

With tears in his eyes, Samuel thanked them both. "You gentlemen, you have given my life a new purpose and meaning. I won't die as a nobody in the shadows, even if only by you two, I will be remembered as a man and not just some unholy being. That means more to me than you can possibly imagine." Samuel shook both Charles's and Jacob's hands and smiled at them. "What do you say fellas, shall we begin? By the way, do either of you have any holy water?"

"Holy water? Does that have an effect on vampires?" Charles was confused by Samuel's strange request.

"It most definitely does, it'll burn like a pot of boiling water. Holy water and crucifixes can hurt and slow us down. Not exactly sure why, but it does the job pretty well. Overheard ya talkin bout garlic, that'll burn if mixed in with water and dumped on the skin or if eaten we'll choke it. Effects are only temporary but makes for a good distraction. The surefire way is to chop off the head and the stake through the heart. The only problem is getting close enough to do either. Most vampires have incredible strength and speed, which makes it difficult to get close to them. But you can use the other methods to slow her down and trap her, then do what you need to do." Samuel felt proud that he was doing something good with his life. For so long, he lived a life in the shadows, hiding and living off of rodents. Now he was in the light, so to speak, and he intended on making the most of it.

"That is some incredible and very useful information. How were you able to gather all of this?" Charles was in awe of everything that Samuel had just told them.

"Well, there was a time when I was much more willing to try and end things myself. I bathed myself in holy water, in garlic water, hell I even mixed them all together and all it did was burn the ever loving shit out of me. After that, I just gave up, I ran away and just hid in the deepest darkest places I could find." Samuel's shame shone through his eyes.

"I am so sorry, my friend. I've only been this creature for a short while but I cannot imagine the loneliness and despair you have felt. I promise you Samuel, soon you will be at peace and the pain you once felt will be a distant memory." Jacob truly felt terrible for Samuel. He knew that he could easily be in Samuels shoes and have similar thoughts and that terrified him more than anything.

Charles felt bad for both Samuel and Jacob, he understood that neither of them chose to become a monster or live this nightmarish life. Like Jacob, Samuel had his own Cassandra who took so much from him, but now they both have something more than just the lonely void. They had each other and Charles. Maybe Samuel would change his mind and join their fight or maybe he is just ready to rest peacefully.

"Samuel, I want you to know that if you choose to join us and take part in this fight that lies ahead of us, you won't be lonely any longer. One day I will die but whether it is soon or in the future, I can assure you that I will make sure you and Jacob are set for as long as I can arrange it. You will have a home and friends to lean on. The choice is yours." Charles felt he owed it to Samuel to offer him that much.

"I appreciate your offer and the kind words from the both of you but my mind is set. So, I ask again, shall we get started."

Charles smiled at his new friend. "Yes sir. Since its light out, I will make the run to the church and acquire the holy water. I'm sure the preacher will be confused but a proper donation to his church will settle that. If you gentlemen could work on making some stakes while I'm gone, that would be very helpful. I shouldn't be gone for more than an hour. I'll bring a couple bottles of whiskey back with me, to keep my guests comfortable." Charles nodded to both men as he headed out.

"That is a man of determination and heart. I hope he truly knows that this fight that you two are preparing for will be dangerous beyond anything he has ever faced. As for you, Jacob, we can work on your abilities as well. From what you've told me and what I've seen, they can be stronger if you want them to be. You use that knife to sharpen those logs into pointed stakes but with a simple thought you can grow your claws and sharpen them to an incredible point."

Samuel looked at his own hands as his nails grew into sharp talons, with a flick of his fingers the wood flew off of the log. He set it down and it was perfectly shaped and sharpened. Jacob smiled and looked down at his hands, he focused on his hands, his nails and he watched as they slowly extended out. He looked up at Samuel and smiled. He grabbed the log and flicked his fingers at the log, wood chips flew all around him. He set the log down and smirked at his handy work.

"Nicely done. With practice and patience, you can carve out intricate detailed designs and sell them. I did that for a while, it was actually fun but a customer saw me do the carvings and I was chased out of town. People can be quite cruel when they are afraid and see something they're not familiar with." Samuel had been fidgeting with a small log while he was talking to Jacob, he looked up, set the piece of wood down and it was the shape of a horse.

"Samuel, that is incredible. I will have to work on my skills, I would love to be able to do that and make money. I see that I truly have a lot to learn. Do you have any other tips or lessons? I don't know what my future holds but I would like to be as prepared as I can be." Jacob was willing to embrace whatever possibilities that the future may have in store for him. He did not know when the confrontation with Cassandra would take place but when it did, he knew that there would be a chance that he would not make it out alive. On the off chance he did survive, he would make sure he spent every moment enjoying life and find ways to protect others from monstrous villains like her.

It had been just over an hour when Charles returned. He was amazed to see the stack of stakes that Jacob and Samuel had made. They had easily made fifty, which was far more than he had expected. Charles had set several jars of holy water on one of the tables in the kitchen area, he also placed two bottles of whiskey at the opposite end.

"Now don't mix up the bottles and accidentally drink the holy water instead of the whiskey." Said Charles with a grin, as both men chuckled. "You guys have definitely surpassed my expectations. I did not expect this many stakes to be prepared. Very nice work,"

"It was actually a quick job. Once Samuel showed me a trick, we were able to knock those out quickly." Jacob smiled at Samuel.

"Eh. All in a day's work, I guess." Samuel smirked.

"How do you want to proceed Samuel? We have the jars of holy water, stakes prepared, I will have the garlic chopped and placed into separate jars with water. Jacob mentioned silver, I was thinking I could put in an order to the town's local gunsmith in town for some silver bullets and a few knives. I'm sure it'll be an odd request but I highly doubt he will refuse it or my money. Is that something that we should look into?" Charles was already calculating out the price for the silver weapons, it wasn't going to be cheap but it would be worth the cost if it worked.

"Silver does hurt us. I suppose, like any weapon plunged into the right area, it will do a decent amount of damage. You do have to keep in mind that we have a really fast healing ability. I have no doubt that the blades can and will slow a vampire down but once it is removed from the body, you will have one pissed off SOB on your ass." Samuel looked at Charles' gun and wondered if a type of silver bullet could be made to fire from it." As much as you probably don't want to, I think this may be one of those ideas we will need to test out. That gun of yours fires lead bullets, it may be possible to fire a bullet made of silver. The only problem is time won't be on your side. Those guns fire only six bullets so in the amount of time it takes to reload, she'll be on you so you need to make each shot count. The knives could possibly be used if she was trapped and unable to attack you. The idea has never been tested, I am willing to give it a try if necessary. Maybe put some horse blankets down to catch the blood."

"You're correct, I do not want to test this one out but I do understand why we need to. Once we have the silver bullets, which should be tomorrow, we can test them. When I head to the gunsmith's shop to place the order, I will pick up some blankets from the general store. Well gentlemen, besides the most permanent methods, I don't think there is a whole lot we can do today. I'd say pop open them bottles of whiskey and enjoy yourselves. I'd stay but the sun will be setting in a couple of hours and I should be home before Cassandra wakes up. I don't want her getting suspicious or anything. Plus, I need to get to the gunsmiths today so he can begin the order. So, I wish you a good evening and a good night. I will see you tomorrow."

Both Jacob and Samuel said goodbye to Charles as he made his way out the door. Charles could hear them clinking the glasses together and saying cheers. It was only a short ride to the gunsmith's shop and Charles was right. He did find the request odd but when Charles offered to pay an extra twenty dollars, on top of the price for the knives and bullets, the gunsmith agreed. He said the order would be ready for pick up in a day or two. He would have it packed up and would be sure to keep the boxes safe for Charles.

When Charles got home, he climbed into the bath to wash up. He wasn't sure if Cassandra would be able to smell either men's scent or the fact that he had been out on his horse today. He put on fresh clothes and had his staff pick up the old clothes and wash them right away. Charles had the kitchen staff begin making dinner while he waited in the study. As he sat there thinking about the day and how grateful he was that Jacob found Samuel, he dozed off in the chair. He dreamt of Cassandra chasing him through the house, as she ran after him she would leave massive scratch marks along the walls. It was only when she finally caught him and was about to rip at his throat that he was startled awake.

He looked up to see Cassandra standing in front of him and he gasped. She was drenched in blood, it was all over her face and dripping from the corners of her mouth. The front of her dress was stained in a deep crimson and he could see the chunks of torn flesh stuck to her nails. She took a looming step towards him and said, "What is the matter Charles?". He jumped up and fell out of his chair.

The moment he hit the floor, his head shot up. He was still in his chair sleeping and he only actually truly woke up when he fell in his nightmare. What remained was that Cassandra was standing there, only she was not covered in flesh and blood. She was clean and her hair was styled.

"Charles, are you ok? It appears you have had a nightmare and scared yourself awake." Cassandra spoke with a soft and concerned tone.

"Yes, I am fine and I did have a nightmare. I was waiting for dinner and I wasn't expecting to fall asleep." Charles shook off the sleepiness and looked at Cassandra.

"What was your nightmare about? It must have been quite intense if it caused you to awaken so abruptly and so out of breath." Cassandra was honestly curious about what could startle Charles so much.

"I was being chased by a creature that was trying to kill me, when it finally caught up to me and was about to land its kill shot I woke up. Or so I thought I did, I awoke to find myself sitting in my chair and the creature was standing in front of me. Blood soaked, torn flesh stuck to its claws and it came after me. I jumped up in my chair, fell to the floor and that's when I really woke up." He was watching her reactions to his description of his nightmares.

"That sounds awful. Did you see the creature clearly or recognize it?" Cassandra was starting to feel bad for her husband and his terrible nightmare.

"Yes. I did see the creature clearly and I did recognize it. It was you!" The words came out of his mouth like daggers to her heart. He could see the hurt and shock on her face.

"Me? Is that how you see me husband? As a monstrous creature trying to kill you?" Cassandra went from empathetic to angry in an instant.

"Is that not how you have portrayed yourself? As an immortal creature that kills others and threatens to change, the one she is supposed to love, into a creature like herself. In a manner that almost seems like the choice is only an illusion because one way or another, you will have your way." He knew he was treading in dangerous waters with his words but he was no longer willing to live in fear of the woman he married.

"Perhaps you have misunderstood me, my love. The choice is yours to make but you should choose your words more carefully. You have wounded my heart and I do not take kindly to being hurt." Cassandra could feel her rage building up from her husband's words.

"Perhaps you should have found a different way of presenting your intentions. The reminder you left on the wall left quite an impression and it is not a positive one." Charles was not backing down and intended to prove his point to her. "Perception, my dear, is everything. Your actions were perceived as hostile and quite threatening, whether that was your intention or not, it was how it was taken and how it looked."

"Well, I see that your courage has emboldened you. It's both refreshing and irritating. If I wanted to threaten you, I would and believe me, you would know it. As far as how my actions were perceived, I did lose my temper and my patience with you. However, in the future, I will make further attempts at controlling my anger. Especially in regards to you." Cassandra was merely telling her husband what she thought he wanted to hear.

"Let's hope that our actions match our words, my love. It's been quite difficult as of late, with Chloe being gone and the terrible accident involving Jacob. There is a heavy weight on my heart and I do not know how much more heartache I can bear." Charles looked her in the eyes as he made his statement. He also wanted to be sure that she had no inclination or suspicion that Jacob was still living and that they were forming a plan to stop her monstrous reign of fear.

<u>Chapter Six</u>

Charles was finishing up his dinner with Cassandra. The staff came, gathered the dirty dishes and cleared the table. Charles could see the look of fear in their eyes as they moved around the table. He felt anger and shame since it was his fault that they were trapped in this horrid nightmare with his monstrous wife.

"Come Cassandra, let's retire to the living room and enjoy the warmth of the fireplace. Perhaps you can tell me more of your past and the life you lived before we met." Charles was trying to find a reason to get her away from the staff so that they could work in peace and not in fear.

"That sounds like a wonderful idea, husband." She got up and followed Charles to the living room. She sat down in her chair that he bought her. He poured her a glass of her favorite wine, which he knew had blood in it. He poured himself a glass of whiskey and sat down in the chair across from her. "I would love to tell you more about myself but first my love, tell me how your day was."

Charles was surprised by her request but he indulged her. "My day was fine, I took my horse out for a ride to the lake. I did some fishing, threw back the few fish I caught, came back home and showered. I took a short nap in my study and then had dinner with you my dear."

"Sounds like you had a nice and relaxing day. I am glad, you certainly deserve it. I recall you saying things have been difficult for you lately. What about my past would you like to know? I've told you the most important parts, the events in between are trivial. I traveled throughout England, went to France and Germany. I lived in Ireland for five years but none of those places ever felt like home. Just empty rooms where I slept. I never loved anyone like I love you, there were a few people that I bonded with and even became friends but eventually they died. Once I accepted the finality of a mortal's existence and how short their lives really were, I began to isolate myself. I kept my interactions brief and I never let anyone get too close. For me, it was easier that way and I didn't have to worry about the heartbreak that followed with the passing of others." Cassandra said in a flat monotone voice.

"That sounds like a very lonely and depressing way to live. To never let someone in or get close to anyone in fear of getting your heart broken. That is no way to live. You must take those chances, whether they are good or bad, it'll help shape the person you want to become. It will help your heart to learn who is worthy of your love and who is not. Walling yourself off from the world just makes for a lonely existence." Charles realized he was going off on a tangent and was basically talking about her. "At least that's what I think but what do I know compared to someone who has probably seen the best and worst of humanity. Forgive me, I let my thoughts run away with my words."

"You are both right and wrong. You're right because I did wall myself up and I did keep the world at bay. I did so because I have seen the hate in the hearts of others and every time it outweighs the love. People hate others who are different from them and even when I hide my true self, they still seem to find flaws to tear me down. They would look at me in disgust because my skin was lighter than theirs or berate me because I was frequently out at night so I must have been a prostitute. I learned that people are so cruel and I learned to keep the garbage and filth of humanity away from my heart. I did eventually let my walls down and when I did, I found you. With you I found a peace that I had never known and that led us to our sweet baby Chloe. When she died part of my heart died with her, perhaps it was the kinder and softer side that she took with her. But that pain was more unbearable than anything I had ever felt, in all the many years I have lived, that pain was the worst." The look of pain and despair was easily seen on her face, so much that she had to turn away from Charles. She did not want him to see her looking weak or vulnerable.

"I'm sorry that you had such a rough and difficult life. I know that you have had a much longer life than I and overall, you have dealt with so much more but I too have had my share of hardships and pain. But I am sure it seems miniscule compared to what you've dealt with. I can't imagine living the life you have lived, from your description it was more pain than enjoyment." Charles looked down at his glass of whiskey and took a slow sip.

"For much of it, it was lonely and painful. I had to learn to live all over again and it took some time to not let others' words affect me. My temper was, at one point, quite terrible and my appetite was insatiable. It has taken many years and lots of work to get to where I am now, believe me when I say that it was not an easy process to endure." Cassandra spoke with confidence and pride.

Charles looked at her and with all his strength he held back the words he wanted to say to her. In his mind, he thought that she was still an animalistic monster who was responsible for the deaths of the three people he cared for the most in this world. He thought that this world, no matter how bad she thought it was, did not deserve to be the hunting grounds for this evil monstrosity. His thoughts were full of hate and disregard for this woman who he once loved. However, the words he spoke, he knew had to be far from what his thoughts were. They had to be kind, soft and caring because one day very soon she would find out that her husband and the boy she tried to kill would be the ones ending her terror. That truth and reality of that moment could not be revealed until the time to act was upon them.

"I see that you have pride in the fact that you have worked so hard and you should be proud of yourself, that level of determination is truly commendable. I raise my glass to you my dear wife and I cheers you." He raised his glass to his wife and drank down his last sip of whiskey. "Would you care for another glass of wine?" He asked as he got up to pour himself another glass of whiskey.

"Yes please. Thank you dear. I appreciate your kindness." She held out her glass for him to take.

"It's my pleasure." He grabbed her glass and set it down next to his as he poured himself more whiskey. He grabbed the bottle of wine that was sitting next to the whiskey decanters, it was a new bottle so he grabbed the wine bottle corkscrew and began twisting it into the cork. Once it was all the way in the cork he gave the opener a hard tug. As the cork and opener popped out, the bottom of the corkscrew slid across the palm of his left hand and cut him. He yelled out in pain as he set the bottle down and quickly grabbed his bandana from his back pocket. He wrapped his hand tightly in an attempt to stop the bleeding.

Out of the corner of his eye, he could see Cassandra sitting there staring at his hand and the blood soaked bandana. She slowly stood up from her chair and took a step towards him. He could see a crazed feral look in her eyes as she slowly moved towards him. He took a couple of steps backwards and called out to her. "Cassandra, what are you doing?"

She blinked several times, looked him in the eyes and reached out to hand him the cloth napkin she had sitting on her lap. She looked at him and took a deep breath. "Are you alright? Do you need me to have someone fetch the doctor?"

He could tell that the sight of his blood had awoken the hunger inside of her, yet she was clearly trying to hold herself back. It aroused his curiosity, after all she had already done, why now was she showing restraint? He turned to leave the room and stopped to look at her. "Thank you for your concern but I will be back in a moment. I am just going to go clean this up and wrap it tighter."

"Yes dear, do clean that up well, you do not want to take the chance that it becomes infected. Then you would have to consider amputation and I know you do not wish to lose your hand. Don't forget, I am still a nurse as well as your wife." Cassandra smiled at him as he turned to head up the stairs to the bathroom to clean up his hand.

She watched Charles go upstairs, and once he was out of sight she looked at the wine bottle. There was a particular aroma coming from it and she knew the scent perfectly, it was blood. When Charles cut himself with the corkscrew he bled into the bottle as well as on the side of it. She walked over to the bottle, picked it up, licked the side clean and took a long slow sip. The wine flowed from the bottle mixing with the blood that he had shed. She knew there was more in blood than just one's life force. It contained a brief look into the person's memories and in his blood she saw something that enraged her. She saw him with two men, one was another vampire and the other was all too familiar. It was Jacob. She had wondered if he had survived their encounter, especially since the undertaker had said his body was stolen. She noticed something was different about him, he too was a vampire. She thought back to the night of the attack and recalled him hitting her with that rock, it was then that she must have bled into his wounds and turned him. She saw the three men and their plans to find a way to kill her and the deal to put Samuel to rest once their "researching" was completed.

Cassandra threw the bottle into the fire and paced the living room. She couldn't believe that Charles, her husband, whom she offered to share eternity with was planning to betray her and kill her. She thought, "How could this mere mortal think that he, of all people, could destroy someone as powerful and cunning as her. He had no idea what kind of battle he was getting himself into nor would he be prepared enough to win." She decided that she would play into his game, if he wanted her dead so badly, she would give him false hope. She would see just how far he was willing to go and at the moment he thought he had won, she would snatch that victory away and deliver him to his death. She would continue to make him think she was still his loving wife and that she had no idea what he was planning.

Charles had poured some whiskey onto his wound and used a piece of cloth to tightly wrap his hand. He had seen the look in her eyes when he was bleeding, she looked as if she wanted to pounce on him and drink him dry. He replayed the scenario in his mind and realized he bled on to the bottle. He finished wrapping his hand and quickly made his way back downstairs. He saw that the bottle was gone and she was sitting in her chair. "What happened to the bottle of wine Cassandra?" He asked with a hint of nervousness in his voice.

"Nothing to be worried about my love, I saw that there was blood on it and I threw it into the fire. Come look, you will see it shattered and cleansed by the flames. I told you, my love, I have learned great restraint over the years. I would not break your trust and drink your blood without your consent. I wouldn't betray you like that Charles." She spoke tenderly to her husband, enough to see that he took a breath of relief.

"I was not worried, I was going to dispose of it and get you a new one. So that we can continue our evening, but since you already took care of that, I will retrieve a new one and open it more cautiously." He smiled and chuckled as he walked to the tension cabinet for a new bottle. In the back of his mind, he did not believe that she didn't take the opportunity to drink his blood.

"Here we go, a nice new bottle just for you my love." Charles opened the bottle, much slower this time and successfully opened it with no new injuries. He poured her a glass, walked it over to her, handed it to her and kissed her on the forehead. "Now let's enjoy this fine evening and warm fire. How's the wine?"

"The wine is delicious, thank you. How is your hand? I hope the wound won't keep you from handling your day to day tasks." Cassandra looked at him and made sure to show some concern so that he would not suspect that she knew what he was up to. She smiled at a thought that crept into her mind, she would make her offer to him once more. Not because she thought he would accept it but she knew it would bother him. She thought maybe he would make a mistake and let some of his true intentions spill out like his blood from that corkscrew. "I don't know if you are aware of this but with my offer to share our lives for eternity, it comes with the ability to heal rapidly. Your hand would be healed in an instant and there would be no scar or lingering pain. It would be like it never happened." She looked over and smiled at him.

"Cassandra, we have been over this several times. I do not want to become a vampire, not now and not ever. Why do you continue to persist with this notion when you already have my answer? I've been more than clear on this topic and still my answer is NO." Charles began to get frustrated with her. "Why tempt ruining a nice evening with a topic that will only bring up anger and irritation. I demand to know why!"

"You demand? Who are you to demand anything from me? You may request and answer, even beg for one but I do not respond to demands. Not even from you Charles. Not now and not ever." She purposely threw his words back at him.

"Fine. I request to know why you continue to bring this up? I request to know why, we cannot simply just live this life together and allow time and nature to take its natural course? Are you so lonely and selfish that you refuse to respect my wishes?" Charles was angry and he let his words cut her deep.

"Lonely and selfish, that is what you think I am? Why is it selfish to want to spend forever with the one you love? With someone who, after decades of nothing, finally makes you feel love and happiness. How is that selfish? That is why I persist and continue. But you wish to grow old and die, so be it. I will not ask again. Not even when you are on your death bed and wishing that you had more time. Consider my offer withdrawn and no longer an option. Take note of my words, when that day comes and it will come, I will not grant you that wish and all you will get from me is a goodbye." Cassandra stood up, set her glass down on the fireplace mantle, and she walked towards him. She kissed him on the lips and said "goodnight". She walked away from Charles and went upstairs to their room.

Charles sat there in the chair, he watched the flames of the fire dance around and he sipped on his glass of whiskey. He knew that what just transpired was merely the beginning of the turmoil that would take place in their home. He had a feeling that she knew something was off with him and it was quite possible that his plans would have to be either changed or sped up.

He would sleep in his study that night because he did not trust Cassandra nor did he want to sleep next to her.

He grabbed a blanket from the study closet and wrapped it around his shoulders. He sat in his chair, propped his feet up and fell asleep. He dreamt of the day he arrived in Wills, he saw the corpses lying around the church and saloon. This time there was something different, he walked over to his wagon and saw something horrific on the floor. It was Edwards' body, covered in blood and torn skin hanging from his bones but he was still alive and awake. He heard a grotesque sound of bones breaking and skin tearing. Crouched down next to him, chomping on his rib cage and slurping blood from their hands was Chloe. She was as he remembered her before she died, so small and fragile. "Hello father, he is delicious. Can you bring me more, I am so hungry and I want more." Her face was in a snarled growling pose, her mouth, stained red from the blood, had two long fangs and she licked her lips so she wouldn't waste a single drop of her meal.

Edward reached out for Charles. "Help me, my friend. P…please kill me."

Charles reached down for the pistol that was strapped to his hip. He pulled the hammer back and aimed it at Edward. With tears in his eyes, he pulled the trigger. The gun fired but nothing happened, no bullet shot out. He tried again and again and again. His voice cracked as he spoke. "I am so sorry Edward. Please forgive me."

Just then Chloe reached up and ripped at Edward's throat. She tore off a chunk of his neck and the blood poured out of his friend like a bottle spilling wine. He couldn't do anything but stand there, frozen in fear, as he watched his friend choke and drown in his own blood. With every cough and gasp for air, he spit out blood and blood would squirt out of the gash on his neck. Charles collapsed and dropped to his knees, tears streamed down his face. As he looked up at Chloe, she sat there staring at him and then she jumped at him.

The moment she tackled him to the ground he fell out of his chair and woke up. He sat up on the floor and saw that the sun had begun to rise. He wiped his face because the tears in his nightmare were actually rolling down his face. He stood up and grabbed the chair as he stumbled with his first step. He walked over to the bathroom and splashed water on his face. He slowly looked up at his reflection and his eyes were bloodshot. He made his way downstairs to the kitchen and asked the kitchen staff to make him some coffee and breakfast. He ate his food and stepped outside with his coffee.

After he finished his coffee, he set the cup down on a table outside and made his way to the stable to get his horse ready to go. He put his saddle on his horse and climbed up. He started making his way to the back house where Jacob and Samuel were staying. He noticed that there was some mild discomfort in his hand from last night's accident with the cork screw. He was grateful that it was his left hand and not his dominant hand, but it was still uncomfortable and painful, nonetheless.

As he approached the house, he noticed the front of a rifle pointing out of the slightly opened door.

"Don't come any closer, I got ya in my sights? State yer name and yer business." Samuel shouted.

"Hold your fire, it's me. It's Charles. I'm getting off my horse and slowly approaching." Charles was not expecting this type of welcome. Something must have spooked them.

"Samuel, put down that damn gun. Come on in Charles." Jacob had taken the rifle away from Samuel and called for him to come in.

Charles made his way into the house, making sure that he didn't open the door too far in order to keep the sunlight out. "Well, that was one hell of a welcome. Where did you get that rifle from?"

Jacob closed the door behind Charles. "We found it in one of the bedroom closets. What happened to your hand? We picked up the scent of your blood as you got nearer."

"That's what I wanted to talk to you both about. I cut it last night while opening a bottle of wine." He went over the events of the night, including Cassandra making her offer again and his suspicions that she drank his blood that was both on the bottle and in it. "I swear she only asked again to get a reaction out of me. She knew that I would say no and that it would anger me."

"This is not good." Samuel said with a look of fear and defeat on his face. "The blood contains everything you are. It stores your memories, your thoughts and whatever it is that makes you "You". If she has drunk even just a small drop then she will most certainly know what we are planning and how we intend to accomplish it." Samuel collapsed into one of the chairs in the living room.

"What do we do now? If she knows the plan then she also knows that I am still alive and that Samuel is helping us." Jacobs' voice trembled.

"That means we will need to either switch up our plan of attack or we will need to speed up the time frame. Either way, and I hate to ask this of you Samuel but will you help us fight her?" Charles knew that he was asking him to delay their arrangement.

"I thought I was already doing that. Now, if you're asking me to wait on finally being able to rest in peace, that's a whole different thing." Samuel looked at both men while he was sitting there, he looked down at the floor. "This really isn't my fight. I agreed to make sure you both were prepared and that was all."

"Samuel I am…" Charles was interrupted by Samuel standing up.

Samuel looked Charles straight in his eyes. "I'm not done. This isn't my fight and it's not what we agreed on. But I suppose by the time this is over I will have what I want. It's about time I stood with men who fought for good and not just for themselves. I will help but if this crazy wife of yours doesn't kill me, I fully expect you to hold up your end of our deal."

"Samuel, you sir are a true friend. I appreciate this more than you can possibly imagine. Thank you so much." Charles reached out and shook Samuel's hand.

Charles began first. "I think we better get to work. We know what we need to do, which is kill Cassandra. We know how to do it, thanks to you fine gentlemen. The only questions that remain are where will we do this and when. My parents used to talk about this island that they would visit and enjoy the beaches. It's down south but by boat it can be accessed easily. They would sail from Georgia down to this island and stay there for about two or three days. My father would explore the caverns while my mother would cook the fish he had caught. I've been thinking this would be the best place."

"How would we get there and what would we need to do to prepare for your arrival?" Jacob sounded nervous.

"We can't exactly sail there ourselves. Who would pilot the ship during the day?" Samuel was curious about this plan as well.

"I can hire a small crew to take you two down there, plus I believe two of the men on house staff are familiar with ships and are aware of our Cassandra problem. I'm sure I would be able to have them accompany you there and come back with the ship to port. They can meet you both in Georgia so there won't be any questions on the way down. Once aboard the ship there shouldn't be any problems." Charles knew this was the only way to get them there ahead of his and Cassandra's arrival.

"I suppose we can work the galley until we arrive, it's in the belly of the ship so the sun won't be a problem. Plus, it gives us legit reasons for not being out on the deck. I have some sailing background so that will come in handy. I will keep Jacob as my assistant so no one will give us a second thought. Just as long as we keep them fed properly." Samuel was proving to be more useful than anticipated.

"Sounds like, between the two of you, the where and how is pretty much covered. I'll make sure we have everything we'll need packed and ready to go. Once night falls, we will have to row to shore and find a cavern to take shelter in. Charles, we will need the weapons, the silver bullets and probably some ropes. We'll also need gloves so we can handle the knives and load the guns without injuring ourselves with the silver. The stakes will be easy to pack since they'll just seem like lumber and the holy water will need to be surrounded by blankets to keep them from breaking. The garlic will be easy enough to get since we'll be working in the kitchen or galley. I think we should move somewhere else, since Cassandra knows we are here. We can break a jar of the water and garlic to cover our scents, in case she decides to come here and inspect the house." Jacob was really stepping up and taking charge of the supplies. He felt he had to do something to be useful, both men have other strengths that he lacked. Packing and labor he excelled in because that is what his father taught him.

"That sounds great, thank you both so much. I'm sure we have plenty of gloves in the stables, be sure to take extras just in case they're needed. I can get whatever you need from town, I still need to pick up the weapons we ordered, we don't wanna leave that there for too long. I was also thinking about purchasing two more pistols and three rifles, just in case we are able to trap her. Though that may be a longshot, I fear that the only way we will get this done will be a face to face fight. Hopefully with the number advantage the odds will be in our favor. We still have some time before we get to that point. I will head into town and send a letter to the captain of my family's ship. He runs our trade schedules so, if I request it, I am sure I can have him make an unscheduled stop wherever I need." Charles was thinking of what to say in the letter to the captain.

"I forgot about your ship, it has been so long since you've traveled on it, I thought maybe you sold it." Jacob said with surprise in his voice.

"I had given it some thought but my father loved sailing on it so I couldn't bear to sell it. I thought for a while that someday I could take Chloe sailing, show her the open sea and all the stars in the sky. At night, in the middle of the ocean, the sky is endless and seems like you are truly looking at eternity." Charles was smiling as he spoke of sailing with Chloe.

"I am sure that Ms. Chloe would have loved that Charles. I can see her smiling and eyes full of wonder as you and her stared up at the sky." Jacobs' eyes watered as he thought about Chloe.

Charles looked over at Jacob and Samuel and smiled. "Ok. Enough of this sappiness. We have a mission to prepare for and we need to be sharp with our wits about us. I'm going to head to town and send my letter to the captain. Here is some money for you gentlemen to spend in town tonight. After tonight we will be on a path that will not allow for any distractions or mistakes. Unfortunately, our time line has been sped up and with rushed plans mistakes are likely, but I know the three of us can and will succeed."

"Ah, very true indeed. When things go too fast, steps are skipped and mistakes in a plan like ours can prove to be fatal. Consistency is key, as long as we all stick to the same plan and don't make any last minute changes, we will be fine. We must keep calm and be level headed no matter what comes our way." Samuel felt confident in Charles's plan.

"Gentlemen, you both have yourselves a good evening. I will keep you updated on any word from the ship's captain. I will grab our supplies from town and figure out how I am going to get Cassandra to agree to get on this ship and sail to the island. She may already have some information from when she tasted my blood last night, so convincing her will not be an easy task. No matter what it takes, I will get it done." Charles was fully determined to get his tasks accomplished.

On his way to town, Charles was trying to figure out a way to convince her to go. He had his suspicions that she was already aware of his intentions, but whether it was all or just some of his plans he did not know. He would have to entice her somehow and even lie to make her want to go on this trip. He knew he had to be convincing or at the very least make it seem like it was her idea to embark on the voyage. Perhaps if he was able to use something from her past it may help to sway her decision. He just had to figure out what he could use that would motivate her to want to sail to an island she's never heard of with her husband who may be planning her death.

All of a sudden he had an idea, he turned his horse around and headed back to Samuel and Jacob as fast as he could. He got to the house and jumped off the horse, he was moving so fast that he almost tripped over the doorway of the house as he ran inside.

"Samuel!" Charles paused to catch his breath. "Do poisons or sedatives work on vampires?" Charles sat in one of the chairs in the living room.

"To be honest with you, I am not sure. We have a faster metabolism than humans, so if it were to work it would have to be an incredibly high dose. I doubt it would kill a vampire but if done at scheduled times it may be possible to keep one asleep for the length of the trip."

Samuel was assuming that it would work, he had never had any real interaction with sedatives or poison.

"If this were to work then we could possibly keep Cassandra asleep for longer than just the time it took to get from Georgia to the island. We could start the process early, in order to make sure we have the correct amounts. There is a good chance that this would hopefully save us from any unnecessary danger." Charles felt bad that he was excited about this fact. Having to kill someone whether they're a terrible monster or not is still murder and that is not an occasion to celebrate. He was more relieved at the thought that he could still keep Jacob safe and maybe even Samuel as well.

"I'm going to talk to the store keeper in town and see if he knows anyone that is familiar or specializes in apothecary. I believe if we can get an ample amount of a sedative or something to induce sleep, we will be much better off. Then the weapons and other supplies can be used for the final steps of our plan. Ok, I am leaving now." Charles was praying that the shop keeper would be able to help him.

During the entire ride to town Charles felt as if someone had been watching him. He looked over his shoulder with a suspicious glare but saw no one. He snapped the horse's reins and the horse started galloping faster. He rode quickly for a bit then abruptly stopped, jumped off the horse and turned around. He unholstered his gun, quickly pulled back the hammer and fired a warning shot. He noticed that someone had slipped back behind one of the trees to his left. He shouted, "Come out and keep your hands where I can see them!"

A woman stepped out onto the road and began to slowly walk towards him. She was in her early twenties or late teens, she was average build and about five foot six inches. She had dark brown hair and brown eyes. She seemed quite athletic, especially since she was able to keep up with him before he sent his horse running down the road. She was wearing tan pants, a black shirt and brown boots. She took a few more steps towards Charles and then she stopped. She raised her hands up so that her finger tips were level with her shoulders. With a look of both fear and embarrassment, the woman just stared at Charles.

Charles was shocked and disappointed that he knew the woman following him. Her name was Erica, she was one of the members of his staff. She had been under his service for the past three years and he never expected that she would be following him. "Erica, why are you following me? Shouldn't you be back at the house or doing something other than following me?"

"I am sorry Charles, I know I shouldn't have been following you but Miss Cassandra said she was worried that you had taken up a mistress. She asked me to follow you for the day and tonight after you went to bed I was to give her a full report of your day. I didn't want to follow you, but I am deathly afraid of her. There are rumors amongst the staff that she killed Jacob and a few other people. I know I owe you so much for hiring me and giving me a home but your wife gives me nightmares and terrifies me. Please forgive me, I will do anything you tell me to do or go wherever you tell me to. Just please do not make me go back home and have to face her. Please!" Erica dropped to her knees, crying and begging him to keep her safe.

Charles was completely caught off guard by her words and actions. Had he been so blind to the fact that he wasn't the only one living with that monster. He had basically condemned everyone under his employment to a life of fear and horror. "Erica, I am truly sorry for what I have put everyone through. It was never my intention to burden you all with Cassandra and her horrors. Forgive me for what I must ask you next. If what you're telling me is true and I help you escape from her, what guarantee do I have that you are not actually working for or with her? I know it seems like an unfair question to ask but she has ways of manipulating people, therefore I must ask."

"As much as I would like to be offended by your question, I can see why you would question my words. My actions do not exactly show that I am trustworthy. However, I have been following you since this morning and I saw Jacob through the window of the house on the far end of the property. He has known me since you first hired me. Take me to him and he will be able to tell you if I am lying or telling the truth. He and I were very close before his accident, he was a very sweet young man and I miss him dearly." Erica spoke of Jacob very softly and with compassion in her voice.

"Well, I suppose there is no point in lying to you, since you've been following me all damn day. Jacob is not as you remember him. Since his supposed accident, which was no accident, he is different. If I take you to him, you may not like what has become of him but I will let you decide that. I will tell you though, if you choose to come with me, you will not be allowed to come back to the house. You will need to stay where I tell you to and if I find out you are lying to me. Let's just say that you will regret that decision. Climb on the back of my horse if you agree to come with me." Charles still had his gun loaded and he knew if she did not agree he would have no choice but to use it.

Erica looked down at the ground and thought. She knew that Cassandra would be furious with her and would come looking for her if she didn't check in tonight. However, that would be the perfect cover, she could go with Charles and learn the location of the weapons. Which is exactly what she was tasked to do and then she could get her reward. "Ok. I will go with you, I refuse to work for that horrible woman. I simply cannot and will not betray your trust anymore. Selfishly, I have missed Jacob so much, so I would love to see him again." Erica smiled at Charles and wondered if he was believing what she was telling him.

"Very well." Charles climbed back onto his horse after holstering his gun. He reached out his hand to Erica. "Climb on up and we will be on our way."

She grabbed his hand, stepped on his boot and swung her leg over the back of the horse. He snapped the reins and took off back towards the house where Jacob and Samuel were. As he approached the house, he saw the shades move over ever so slightly. He knew they were aware of his approaching and his unexpected visitor. As he got off the horse and helped Erica down, he could hear Samuel yelling to him.

"What's going on Charles? Why have you brought her here?"

"We're coming in." was Charles's only response.

He walked through the door and stepped aside so that Jacob could see Erica. His eyes widened with shock and curiosity. "Erica, what are you doing here? Charles, why is she here?"

"Do you want the long story or the short version?" Charles asked.

Both men responded at the same time. "The short version."

"Well, basically, she was Cassandra's spy. I caught her following me as I was heading into town from here." Charles told them what Erica had said about Cassandra and her begging him to help her escape.

"Erica, it's good to see you. I have missed our talks and spending time with you but you should not have gotten yourself involved with Cassandra. She is evil and she made me into a creature like her." Jacobs' voice resonated with anger.

"A creature like me as well, though I have not had the unfortunate privilege of meeting this Cassandra. I am Samuel." Samuel introduced himself.

"It's a pleasure to meet you Samuel. And I'm sorry Jacob, I didn't have a choice. I was terrified she was going to hurt me or kill me. I had to agree to help her, after what happened to you, everyone at home is terrified to make the wrong move. We fear that we'll become her next meal or be murdered for her demented enjoyment." She knew she only had to convince Jacob. If she could do that, he would protect her and vouch for her with Charles and Samuel.

"I do understand that fear, but there is always a choice to be made and you made the wrong one. I was never given a choice, I was attacked and hunted down like a dog. I was murdered by that evil woman and left for dead. Unfortunately for me, the only time I was able to defend myself made me into a creature like her. I struck her with a rock and she bled unintentionally into the wounds that she made. Now I am a vampire like her." As Jacob watched Erica, he noticed that she had a nervous look on her. He couldn't tell if it was because of him and Samuel or because she had been caught but something was off about her.

Samuel was watching as Jacob told Erica what had happened between himself and Cassandra. Instead of looking sad or distraught, she had a look that he could tell Jacob was picking up on. She looked more amused and entertained by his words, enthralled by the events leading to his demise. "There is one easy, painless and sure way to find out if the young miss here is lying or telling the truth." Samuel looked at Jacob and Charles and then at Charles's hand, they nodded. At that point Samuel knew both men understood what he was talking about.

Erica stood there, she turned to look at all three men and stopped at Samuel. "I will do it, I will do whatever is necessary to prove that I have no intentions of working for or with her."

"Hold out your hand." Samuel said to Erica.

Erica did as she was told. She held out her left hand and watched Samuel raise his hand. His finger nails extend and come to a point. Her eyes widened and she held her breath. Samuel closed his hand, leaving only his index finger out and quickly tapped her index finger with his pointed nail. She watched a small bubble of blood form over the spot where he poked her finger. Samuel licked his nail and closed his eyes.

Samuel took a step back and spit on the floor. "What is the reward for finding the weapons?"

"What?" Erica's eyes filled with terror. "H.. How do you know about that?"

"The blood doesn't lie. Your words and actions are quite a show of betrayal and deceit. Your blood has told me that you plan to give us up to Cassandra. You know that when you do not show tonight, she will come looking for you and she will find us." Samuel glared at her in anger.

Jacob spoke. "Well, I wasn't expecting that level of betrayal. Erica, I am deeply and truly disappointed. After everything you've heard around the estate, what she has done to me and you still chose to serve her. What could she have offered you that is worth hurting the people who care for you?"

"She offered her the same thing she had offered me, immortality, strength and power. I know now how you were able to keep up with me while I was on my horse. She gave you a taste of her blood, didn't she?" Charles couldn't believe that Cassandra would go this far, to offer to turn someone just to get information on his activities. "You don't really believe her, do you? She'll never truly make you into a vampire like her. If anything, the moment you give her the information that she tasked you to obtain, she will kill you. Without hesitation and without regret. I can promise you that."

"How do you know? She says that you have abandoned her, that you only wish to kill her and run off to find a new wife and family. What reasons would she have to lie to me or to want to kill me? I have done nothing to her or against her." Erica was now panicking.

"You just don't get it do you? She is evil, she needs no reason to commit heinous murders other than because she enjoys it. That is why she must be stopped. So, you decide to side with Cassandra and then to lie to us about it, it leaves us with quite a problem. There seems to be only two logical solutions here. One solution, the one you really won't like, we kill you and burn your body. This eliminates any suspicion from Cassandra because it looks like you ran off. The second option, which will depend on my friends here, is to let you live. Doing so would mean you would be confined to our company at all times but it would also depend on our ability to trust you. Honestly at this moment, the first choice seems to be the safer and most logical. But I would like to hear what Jacob and Samuel have to say." Charles wanted to be merciful but at the same time their safety was his top priority.

Samuel looked at both men and gave his opinion. "I have no ties to this woman. So, if killing her keeps us safe and our plan on track, I will do it to save you both from having her death on your conscience. At the same time, it would be useful to have someone around to work for us and assist us with the preparations."

Jacob looked at Erica with pain in his eyes. "I am truly heartbroken by your actions Erica. I never thought you would be the one to betray me, especially by working with the person who tried to end my life. I don't know if I can trust you anymore but I do know that I cannot kill you. I refuse to do so. Charles, whatever you and Samuel decide, I will respect your decision."

Erica dropped to the floor in tears. "I am so sorry Jacob. I never knew what she was capable of, yes everyone talked about it, but I never wanted to believe it. It seemed more likely that Charles was, as she said, trying to replace her than her being a murderous monster. Yes she did offer to make me like her and up until now I wanted that power and strength. I was so tired of being the helpless girl who served people. I wanted to be my own woman, strong and proud, able to fend for myself. To be able to protect myself and not rely on someone else. Please take pity on me. Let me live. I will do as I am told and do what's asked of me." She truly did not want to die and after hearing Jacobs story, she wanted to be on the right side of this issue.

Erica knelt in the middle of the room, crying and regretting her decisions. "W…what if Samuel or Jacob tests my blood if needed. They will be able to tell if I've kept up my end of our bargain. I promise that I am done with helping her. Please."

"That sounds reasonable to me. Charles, Jacob what do you boys think?" asked Samuel.

Jacob spoke next. "I'm fine with that. But, Erica, you have a lot of work to do to earn my trust back." Jacob walked out of the room.

"I'm fine with that but we will need a way to cover her scent. Cassandra will come looking for her and if she comes here, you both will be dead along with her and then me." Charles looked at Samuel. "Is there any way to cover her scent?"

"Of course there is, but it's not pleasant." Samuel smiled. "We can cover her in horse shit for the night. Tomorrow we can get her cleaned up and find somewhere new for us to stay. Maybe something on the other side of town?"

"Really? Horse shit? That's disgusting. Glad she'll be staying with you. Jacob, are you OK with this?" Charles could see that Jacob was not entirely pleased with his former friend.

"At the moment, No. But I will be. Especially if I get to help smear the shit on her, that should help ease some of the hurt feelings. Just not all of them." Jacob smirked for a moment but went back to the emotionless state as the brief moment of humor passed.

"OK. That seems to be settled for now. I am going to get that letter sent and head back home. Lord knows I don't want to go back there but I won't be chased out of my own home by her." He headed to the door and opened it just enough to exit. As he closed the door he yelled back to Jacob and Samuel. "Looks like my horse left ya boys something fresh. Enjoy."

Charles laughed as he mounted his horse and headed into town. He snapped the reins and took off in hopes of making it to town before nightfall. He thought about Erica and wondered if Cassandra had enticed anyone else to betray him and be her spy. He knew he would have to be more cautious and pay more attention to those around him. He didn't want to ruin the one chance he had to end her.

Charles got to town and went to the general store first to talk to the shop keeper. "Excuse me sir, I was wondering if you knew anyone who was familiar with apothecary."

The shop keeper looked at him for a moment. "What do you need someone like that for?" He asked suspiciously.

"Well, my wife has trouble sleeping and a colleague of mine told me that I should inquire about someone who studies apothecary." Charles had hoped that was enough information to convince the shop keeper to help him.

"My wife had the same problem. I tried an extra glass of wine at dinner but it didn't help. There is someone who can help you, she has a room above the bar and is quite knowledgeable. I will let her know to expect you. Is there anything else I can get for you?" Asked the shop keeper.

"As a matter of fact, there is. I am going to need two pistols, three hunting rifles and the ammunition to go with. I'll also need about two ropes about ten feet each, 5 bottles of wine, a case of whiskey and three bed rolls. I don't need them today but I would like to pick up the supplies tomorrow." Charles pulled out his money and paid the shop keeper. He also gave him a tip for the extra information.

"Very well sir. I will see you tomorrow and I will have everything packed up and ready for pick up. Have a good evening. See you tomorrow." The shop keeper smiled and waved to Charles as he left the store.

Charles decided to head back home. The sun was beginning to set and he wanted to get washed up before

Cassandra began questioning him about his day. He knew he would have to send one of his staff to deliver the letter to the ship's captain. That person would need to be trustworthy and would have to be paid well in order to make sure they didn't just run off. He thought about what he'd say in the letter and he knew that the voyage would need to be kept quiet.

As he approached the house he noticed that it no longer looked like a home to him. With all the death and darkness that emanated from the building, it felt more like a prison. He was a captive in his own home, he couldn't just up and leave because there were so many people who worked for him and depended on him. He dreaded coming home and even more the company he lived with.

He took his horse to the stable and gave the reins to the stable boy. He began walking to the house and opened the back door. He headed to the bathroom to get washed up. He left his clothes with the house maid to get washed and put on fresh ones. He was hungry but he did not want to eat with Cassandra tonight. He had the kitchen staff make a small dinner. They left a plate out for Cassandra and he ate his in his study. After he ate, he fell asleep in his chair.

Cassandra came down stairs and saw her plate waiting for her on the table. She asked the staff if they had seen Charles and they told her he was in his study. She went upstairs wondering why he hadn't eaten with her. When she opened the door, she saw Charles fast asleep in his chair. She walked in and covered him with a blanket. She returned downstairs and ate her dinner in silence.

Once she finished, she began looking for Erica. She was curious to know what her husband had been up to that made him so tired. As she wandered the property searching for the girl, she wondered if she decided to just run off. Cassandra checked all the rooms and asked every staff member that she came across if they had seen Erica. Not a single person had seen her. Cassandra became furious and stormed out the front door. She ran around the property but was unable to pick up the girl's scent. She came to rest at a tree and swung her clawed nails at it. Bark flew off as the wood of the tree splintered in the air.

Cassandra looked back at the house. She raced back inside and went to Charles's study. She silently walked towards him, she sniffed the air around him but could only smell him. There was no hint of Erica or anyone else. He barely smelt of the outside air, though she did notice a faint scent of his whiskey. She left the room and glared at him from the door. She thought either he was quite clever and was able to hide her or he was just worn from the day and in need of some rest.

She left the study and proceeded to their room. She grabbed her journal and began writing. "My spy has disappeared. She was either too cowardly to do the task I set for her or she was discovered by Charles. I doubt he had the stomach to kill her, he may have had one of his little puppets dispose of her. Unless she betrayed me, though she seemed truly committed to the task. I had no true intentions of turning her but if she had shown true courage and dedication, I may have reconsidered. I wonder if he is actually willing to do what is necessary to try and kill me. Will he have the stones to pull it off? I already know what he does so unless he begs me to reconsider my offer to join me in eternity, I will be forced to make a meal out of my dear husband. At least this one will leave me with a home and a fortune to sustain me for a couple of decades. Time will tell, I know vengeance is in his heart for what I did to Jacob. I need to find Jacob and this stranger that they are working with. Perhaps I can sway the stranger to work for me. Then once Charles is dead I will kill him and finish what I started with Jacob. I will enjoy killing that wretched boy again but this time there will be no coming back for him. Only the empty darkness of death."

"I dreamt of my darling Chloe again. How I miss her, I know we will be reunited one day but until then I will hold her in my heart. In my dream I was teaching her how to hunt and how to feed. She was truly gifted, she had speed faster than my own and strength to match me. Her beauty put all others to shame and her fear she imposed was that of legends. She even made me a bit jealous."

She put her journal away and proceeded to the living room to sit in front of the fireplace. She let the warmth wash over her and she closed her eyes. She drifted off to sleep and awoke in a strange place. It looked dark and was extremely quiet. She went to move but was trapped. She was in a coffin, she tried to push on the lid with all her strength but it did not budge. She banged and kicked at the sides of the coffin but was unable to free herself. She screamed, as loud as she could possibly scream but no one came to help her. She was trapped, confined to a small tiny space and no one was coming to help her. She tried to scream again but this time she woke up. She sat up, breathing deep and fast. She looked around and saw no one. "What was that?" She asked herself. Did she have a

premonition of what was to come or was it just a
nightmare?

<u>**Chapter Seven**</u>

Charles was already heading to town to meet up with one of his house staff named John. John had worked for Charles's family for about fifteen years. Out of everyone Charles knew, John was one of the few he truly trusted. He was also a former sailor and a friend to the Captain of Charles's family's ship. He asked John to meet him in town at one of the restaurants for coffee and to go over a very sensitive matter. John was also close to Edward and Jacob, when Charles came home to bury Edward, he was heartbroken. Then when the "accident" with Jacob happened John was wanting to leave the house because he knew that Cassandra was to blame. Charles was able to persuade John to stay but he was given more traveling duties and would do most of the shopping for supplies and foods.

Charles had gotten to the restaurant and chose a table closer to the back to avoid too many eyes on them or ears listening to their conversation. Charles was unsure if Cassandra had recruited any more spies and he didn't want to take any chances. When John walked in he saw where Charles was sitting and he chuckled to himself.

"Are you sure you don't want a table in the kitchen? It's further away from the windows than this table and closer to the food." John laughed as he shook Charles's hand.

"I'm glad you're in such a good mood today John. I think I may be able to either help keep that good mood going for a while longer or possibly make the day a bit more serious." Said Charles as both men sat down.

"Hmm… I'm intrigued. Please continue." John waited patiently for Charles to explain himself.

"I know that you are aware of the on-going problem that is my wife, Cassandra, and the horrific events that have transpired while she's been living in the estate." Charles watched the look on John's face go from happy to stern.

"I do hope you are going somewhere with this fast Charles. You know how I feel about the matter." John was clearly not happy with Charles.

"I am and I am fully aware of your sentiments. I am getting to the point, I just require some patience." Charles stopped as the server came over to pour him and John some coffee. Charles smiled at her as she walked away. "As I was saying, in regard to the Cassandra issue, I am in need of your help. Are you still in contact with the captain of my family's ship?"

"Yes I am. The captain, whose name is James Wells, is a good friend of mine. He recently offered me a place on the ship, just in case I wanted to return to the open seas and leave the land life behind. Why do you ask?" John was curious about Charles's question and getting impatient about the details.

"This must remain between you and I. Absolutely no one at the estate can be told of these plans and if you agree, you will need to temporarily stay at the INN up the road." Charles sighed, he knew that once he disclosed the details to John there would be no going back. "I have been working on a plan to rid us of Cassandra, the main problem is that she is not an ordinary woman. She is a monster that lives off of the blood of others. She, as she called herself, is a vampire." Charles sat there watching John digest what he had just heard.

"A vampire? Firstly, there is no such thing as a vampire, it's a tale told to children to keep them in bed at night. Secondly, as much as I believe she's to blame for Jacob's death, you should be ashamed of yourself for having to come up with such a ridiculous story. Be a man and deal with your personal life." John was irate with Charles and his tone definitely made that clear.

Charles, now angry, decided to share with John much more than he intended. "Sir, you need to watch your tone with me. For one, I have never once lied to you and you know that's the damn truth. What you don't know or understand is that not only is Cassandra responsible for Jacob's death but she is the monster that murdered his father. The massacre that happened in Wills was done by her. She is cursed and has abilities that the devil himself must have given her. I have seen first-hand that she is a cruel monster. The marks on the wall in the house were done by her, with her own hands. Tell me John, what reason would I have to lie to you about this?"

John sat there speechless, part of him wanted to believe this was just some elaborate lie but as Charles said he had never lied to him. "Say I do believe you and this story. What proof do you have? Besides the damages on the wall in the house. And more importantly, what does all of this have to do with me?"

"You want proof? I can give you proof but only if you are agreeing to help me if it is legit." Charles was trying to calm himself down.

"OK. I agree to help, but if you are making all this up, you will be sorry." John reached out his hand for Charles to shake and make the deal.

Charles looked at him, directly into his eyes, and shook his hand. "Now that that's settled, I will continue. Once you see your proof, I will need you to go and talk to Captain James. I need to set up two trips to a location south of Florida. The first trip will be a supply run and passage for my associates, they will need to drop off during the night and will be working in the gallcy during their trip. The second trip will be Cassandra and myself. The return trip home will be needed a few days later and will be for myself and possibly two others. I have already begun rounding up the supplies that will be delivered with my associates. Is this something you can arrange for me?"

"Provided that everything checks out, yes I should be able to do that. Plus, it's your ship. I don't really see it being a problem. Now if you want the crew to be completely tight-lipped, they may need some compensation. As far as I am concerned, I will only need money for the trip to the ship, for meals and for a place to sleep. Is there anything else you will need?" John was suspicious of Charles's plan.

"Yes. A couple things that are outside of the ship stuff. Once you return from talking to the captain, I will need you to take someone that you trust completely to return and oversee the preparations. I will be sending someone with you then that you must keep a close eye on, you know this person and they were initially working with Cassandra. They have sworn to do as we need without question or hesitation. Once this is done, no matter the outcome, I may need you to take over things at the estate. I fear that I may not return but if I do, I will need someone that I trust whole heartedly to take care of the staff and our home." Charles had a solemn look on his face because he knew that if it meant his life he would give it to make sure that no one else would fall to Cassandra.

John looked worried as he listened to Charles' words. "Those sound like the last wishes of a dying man. Should that be needed, I will do as you ask and take care of everything. As far as this person who chose to help Cassandra, I will watch over them but at the first sign of any betrayal, I will do what is necessary to ensure the safety of everyone on that ship. Now that we have gone over what I assume are all of the details, where is this proof that you spoke of?"

"Let me first say a couple more things please. Thank you for doing this John. I know I am asking a lot of you and I hope you know there is no one I trust more to handle this. I'm sure you're thinking that I have lost my mind but very soon those thoughts will be put to rest. My proof is in the house south of the estate in the old house that's been empty for years. I will travel with you there so you won't be scared of what you find. It is someone you are familiar with and at first you will be in shock but you will need to be calm and keep your wits about you. After that, you will need to begin your trip to see Captain James." Charles was a bit concerned with how John would react when he sees Jacob alive and his current condition.

"Afraid? It takes an awful lot to scare me Charles and I am sure you know this. I will do my best to keep my demeanor calm and stable. Shall we leave now? I am a bit anxious to see this proof." John was beginning to stand up so they could leave.

"Yes, let's get on with this so we can get things in motion." Charles got up, left some money on the table for the coffee and the waitress and they left the restaurant.

Both men climbed on their horses and began making their way to the old house. It was a long quiet ride, neither one of them spoke until they approached the house.

Charles dismounted from his horse first as he saw the door slightly open. "It's me, Charles, keep that damn shotgun off of me. This man is with me, he is here to help us."

Samuel yelled out to them. "Alright, come on in."

John looked over at Charles as he dismounted. "This is a bit suspicious Charles. I trust that I won't be shot or harmed by this person."

Jacob yelled out to John. "It is safe John, please come in."

John instantly knew the voice that was talking to him. He looked at Charles in disbelief. "Charles, that's Jacob's voice, how can that be?"

"I know John. Let's go inside so we can explain everything." Charles was relieved that John recognized Jacob's voice and he could see the fear creeping into his eyes. "Keep calm John" Charles said as they made their way inside of the house.

Charles opened the door enough for him and John to enter the house. The moment they entered and closed the door, John stood there frozen as he looked at Jacob. In a blink of his eye, John walked up to Jacob and hugged him.

"I…I thought you were dead. I saw your body that night and it was ravaged and covered in blood. I helped load your lifeless body into the undertaker's wagon. How is this possible Jacob?" John spoke in disbelief and confusion.

Jacob explained the events of that night and how in his one act of defense, Cassandra bled into his wounds turning him into a creature like her. Jacob could still see that John was having a hard time believing their words. "John, you saw my wounds that night, how do you explain this?" Jacob lifted his shirt and bared his chest. The wounds that should have left massive scars were completely gone.

John stepped forward and felt Jacob's chest. "There is nothing there. I saw them, they looked as if a wild animal had ripped you open." John stopped and thought about the marks on the wall in the main house. "They looked like the marks I saw in the house. Charles, you weren't lying. I am sorry I doubted you and what you told me. Give me a moment to gather myself and I will go see Captain James." John sat down in the chair in the living room. He looked over at the other man in the room. "My apologies sir, I am John." John held his hand out to shake Samuel's hand.

Samuel stepped forward and shook John's hand. "Pleasure to meet you John, I'm Samuel. Not to add to your disbelief but I am a creature like Jacob. The term is vampire actually but it's not that important. I'm sure you know this lady here in the kitchen."

Erica stepped out of the kitchen and looked at him. "Hello John."

He looked at her then looked at Charles. "Is this the person that you spoke of, who was working with Cassandra? Is she a vampire too?"

Erica spoke up. "No, I am not a vampire but I was working with her until I saw Jacob was still alive. I am working on earning the trust I once had with Charles and Jacob."

Looking at her with disappointment. "I see, you can add me to that list as well. Young lady, this man has done so much for you, to betray him like you did is unforgivable. The simple fact that these men have offered this opportunity for redemption speaks volumes to the type of men they are. You should be very thankful and make it your priority to keep your word to them. I don't think I would be as forgiving as them."

"I understand and I am very grateful to them." Erica said with tears in her eyes.

"Ok Charles. I am ready to get started on my part of this." John stood up and shook all three men's hands. He and Charles made their way to the door.

Charles said goodbye to Samuel and Erica. He gave Jacob some money to find a room at an inn in a nearby town. He wanted them to start getting what they could ready for their trip and to be further away from Cassandra.

Charles and John stood outside at their horses and spoke about John beginning his trip.

"I never knew such a creature like Cassandra could exist and that she could make others like her. I've heard stories of such creatures but I always assumed they were just that, stories. Things to scare children to make them go to bed without any problems. My god, the horrors you must have seen living with her. I am sorry my friend." John looked down and sighed.

"Thank you John but that is why I need to end this. The world will be a better and safer place with her gone. I need you to understand my level of commitment to this plan, I will do whatever it takes to see this through. I don't care if my life is required to accomplish this, I will gladly give it to keep you all safe. There is one last thing that I will ask of you but once we have secured the trips I will tell you what it is." Charles shook John's hand and gave him an ample amount of money to complete his trip. "Also, when you return please let me know how much will be needed for the crew's secrecy."

Surprised by the amount of money Charles had just handed him, John tried to give some of it back. "This is entirely way too much money."

"I want to make sure anything you may need is taken care of and that you have enough to sway Captain James to help us and be discreet. And yes, I know it is my ship but I do not own the captain or his crew." Charles was covering all possible outcomes and he wanted John to be able to travel comfortably.

John mounted his horse, looked at Charles, tipped his hat to say goodbye and began his journey to see Captain James. In his mind he was still thinking about Jacob and the events that he had survived. The whole thing seemed absurd and far-fetched, if he hadn't seen him with his own eyes he never would have believed it.

Charles climbed up onto his horse and headed to see the person the shop keeper had told him about that could supply him with the sedatives that he needed. Once Charles arrived at the bar, he approached the bar tender and asked about the person the shop keeper spoke of. The bartender pointed to the second door at the top of the stairs, stated that was her room, and her name is Carolyn. Charles made his way upstairs and knocked on the door.

"Excuse me Miss Carolyn, my name is Charles, the shop keeper said that you could help me with something." said Charles through the door.

"One moment please." She replied back.

Charles could hear some rustling around and footsteps heading to the door. As she opened the door, he was shocked by what he saw. She was a young beautiful woman, she had a sun-kissed caramel color skin tone, brown eyes and she was about five foot five inches tall. She had an athletic frame and a warm smile. Charles was awestruck by her beauty.

"Sir, was there something I could help you with?" She smiled as she spoke to him.

"Yes, my apologies for staring ma'am, the umm… the shop keeper informed me that you practice apothecary. Is that correct?" Charles was trying to gather himself to compose himself respectfully.

"Ah, yes I do. He mentioned that you may be stopping by to see me about something to help your wife get some restful sleep. Is that correct?" She asked him.

"That is correct. Sorry I am not usually this out of sorts. I guess I wasn't expecting you to look as you do. I assumed I would be talking to a much older woman and not as beautiful as you." He was still stammering over his words and felt a bit childish for the moment.

"I'm flattered sir, but I believe you are here for your wife, not me. Please come in and do not touch any of the bottles. Some things in here can kill you with a single drop

on your skin." She slyly smirked at him as she led him into
the room.

"Got it. Don't touch anything." He followed her into
the room and closed the door behind him.

"Precisely. So why don't you explain to me exactly
what you're needing, how much you'll need and then we
can talk about prices." Said Carolyn.

"Right. So, my wife, Cassandra, has been having
trouble sleeping. She wakes up several times throughout
the night and sometimes she is just up all night because she
is unable to fall asleep. So, what I need is something that'll
help her to fall asleep and stay asleep for the night. A glass
of wine isn't doing it for her anymore, even two glasses
doesn't help." Charles let out a nervous laugh.

"I see. Normally the person needing the medicine is
here so I can adjust the amounts properly. I am going to be
honest with you, something about this transaction seems
off. Are there any details that you are withholding from
me?" She asked suspiciously.

"What exactly do you need to know? I can answer
any questions that you may have." Charles responded
coarsely.

"Firstly, why is your wife not present? Second, why are you so defensive? I am meant no harm with my questions, I am just used to doing things a certain way. With your wife not here and I can only take you on your word that this is indeed for her to sleep. I do not know you sir, how do I know that your intentions are genuine and not to do harm? You must understand, this business is my life's work and it has been passed down to me from the women in my family." Carolyn was not willing to jeopardize her reputation for a stranger.

"My apologies ma'am. I am a bit on edge and it has been quite hectic at home. She is not here because she has a condition that causes her to react to sunlight. Due to that illness I chose to come here, in her place, to get her something to help her sleep. I understand that this is your livelihood and a family business but if you are willing to help me, I would be extremely appreciative. I can assure you that my intentions are well placed." He knew his words weren't entirely truthful but they did have some truth to them. His idea meant that he would be protecting so many others from becoming Cassandra's prey.

"I am going to take your word sir, but I beg of you, please do not make me regret this decision. I will need her approximate height and weight in order to make sure I get the amounts correct." She was reluctant to proceed but she had this feeling about him, she wasn't sure what it was but she felt that he had a good heart.

"She is roughly five foot nine inches tall and her weight is somewhere around one hundred and sixty-five pounds." Charles realized that Carolyn was shorter than Cassandra, but the way her frame was built, made her quite appealing. "What does height and weight have to do with your products?"

"Well, if I was making this for a man who was taller and heavier than you I would have to use more chemicals than if it was for a thin framed woman. If you gave the higher amount to a smaller person, it could kill them or have some lasting effects that would be unfavorable. Now, it will make a difference on whether the medication is swallowed or if it will be given by injection. Injection works faster and has a longer effect, by swallowing it your stomach acids will weaken the formula. This is all information that I have learned over the years, from my grandmother and mother, as well as from medicine men that lived with Native American tribes." She was mixing different chemicals and powders into a glass bowl that was sitting over a small ceramic bowl that she had made a fire in.

Charles was fascinated by Carolyn and her knowledge about the chemicals she was working with. She moved so fluidly, grabbing and exchanging chemicals and substances. He just sat there watching her, watching her hands as she worked and the intense look of concentration on her face. "What kind of things did the medicine men have to teach? I'd imagine they would have some interesting methods." He was trying to make small talk but felt like he was still tripping over his words.

"Interesting indeed. They believe in supernatural forces that terrorize people. Some of the medicines supposedly protect the person taking them from being taken over or turned into creatures that roam the night. Personally, I have never seen these creatures but I do believe they exist." Carolyn had stopped mixing to watch Charles's reaction. To her surprise he was listening intensely to her.

"You do? Just out of curiosity, has anyone ever asked you to make them something to protect them from something like a vampire?" Charles was never about asking her that but if he could find something to give him protection from Cassandra, then he had no choice but to ask.

Carolyn raised her eyebrows in surprise at his question. "As a matter of fact, yes. Once, about a year ago, a man sought me out to make him something to protect him from a vampire that was pursuing him. After I made it, I never heard from him again. That's a very specific creature to ask about. Are you troubled by a vampire?"

Charles didn't know how to respond. He could either lie or take a chance and tell her. He sat there for a moment contemplating his decision and what he would say to her. He looked up at her, he looked directly into her eyes and decided that he would tell her but withhold some of the details.

"If I tell you this, can you please promise to keep it to yourself." Charles stood up from the chair and extended his hand forward. If she shook his hand, he would take it as a confirmation of her secrecy.

Carolyn moved forward, towards Charles, and shook his hand. "You have my word that I will not utter a word of what you say to anyone."

He let out a sigh of relief and hesitation. "Thank you. Have you heard of the massacre that took place in Wills?"

"Yes. My cousin worked at the saloon in Wills and he was one of the many townspeople that was butchered there. We were very close and it was difficult for me after I found out it happened. I always thought that the whole incident was strange and that something, not someone, killed all those people." She said with sadness in her voice.

"I am truly sorry to hear that, please accept my condolences. I believe that massacre was the work of a vampire and if I am correct, that same vampire has been following me for the past several years." It took a lot for him not to say that he believed his wife was the vampire responsible for Wills.

"Following you? How does something like that just follow you and not kill you or make a meal out of you? That doesn't make sense to me." Carolyn was having a difficult time believing what Charles was telling her.

"I have often wondered the same thing. There have been many sleepless nights that I have just laid in bed waiting for her to finally come for me." Charles got lost in his words.

"Her? Why did you say her? I'm beginning to think you are keeping a lot more from me than just why your wife isn't here." Her suspicions were beginning to change in regard to Charles's honesty. "I think you know more about this vampire that you are sharing sir and to be upfront with you, I am losing my patience with your lies."

Charles had backed himself into a corner, he had to decide if he was going to tell her the truth or risk losing the sedatives he needed more lies. "I believe my wife is the creature responsible for the massacre."

Carolyn stumbled backwards as she stepped away from Charles. "What? How are you married to a vampire and not one yourself? Why do you think she's responsible?"

Charles looked at her with a curious stare. "You seem OK with the fact that I basically stated that my wife is a vampire."

Carolyn stammered. "No. Don't shift the conversation onto me. I demand answers before I say anything else or even consider helping you."

"Fine. She did not tell me she was a vampire before we married. I simply believed that she had a supposed sun allergy. Before her, I never knew such creatures could exist. She admitted to me that she was a vampire after our daughter died. She never confessed to the massacre but as I began thinking about it I came to that conclusion. The timing of when we met and when the massacre happened was barely a day apart. Plus, what are the chances that another vampire was around to do that when she was there, it made no sense to me. The sedatives that I have requested are not to help her sleep but to keep her asleep while I transport her somewhere." Charles could not believe that he was telling this stranger all of this but he desperately needed the sedatives and she was his only hope in getting them.

"As I told you, you're not the first person who has known that vampires exist. You're just the first one who was married to one and living with one. You are truly lucky to be alive, I have never heard of a vampire marrying a human and not turning them into a creature themselves. How do you expect me to help the husband of the vampire that has caused my family such pain and grief." Carolyn was slowly moving closer to her suitcase, she had a gun stored in there in case she ever needed to defend herself from an unruly customer.

"I desperately need your help Carolyn. This monster has taken one of my closest friends, his son and my daughter from me. I fear that soon enough she will lose her patience with me and either kill me or turn me. Then I will not be able to protect anyone from her insatiable hunger and unending need to kill. She has offered me the chance to join her and become just like her, I have no desire to become a monster like her." Charles had stood up from the chair he was sitting in and was now standing directly in front of Carolyn. "Please help me so that I may avenge those she has murdered and stop her from harming anyone else."

Carolyn stood there looking into his eyes, she could see the look of a desperate man with the intentions of doing something incredibly dangerous. "I will help you Charles, but do not claim that you are doing all of this for the memory of people you did not know. Admit that this is also in some part for yourself, own your decision and then I will help you. Do that and I will give you what you need to keep the beast asleep until you can do what needs to be done."

"You're right, I am doing this mostly for myself. I do not wish to live in fear anymore. Every day I go to sleep praying that I wake up. Every day I fear that the moment she sees me, she is going to attack me and turn me into a monster like her. Every day I am tired of being tired. I cannot live this way anymore and yes I do wish to spare others the fear that I live with every day." Charles literally bared his soul to her in hopes that she would still help him.

His words brought tears to her eyes and stirred a feeling that she could not contain. She moved towards him, placed her hands gently on each side of his face and she kissed him. She moved back slowly and looked him in the eyes. "I…I'm sorry, I should not have done that. Your words touched me and I felt your sorrow. I will help you and I will do so free of charge. I will obviously adjust the potency of the sedative, you will need to administer it more frequently since her system will run through it faster than a normal person would." She was blushing from kissing Charles and her body was on fire because she wanted to kiss him again.

Charles could not believe what had just happened, he was at a loss for words because she was a very beautiful and attractive woman. However, he never thought she would be so forward and kiss him. He wasn't sure if he should be upset, ashamed or excited. The more he thought about it, the more he wanted to kiss her some more.

He said her name and as she turned to look at him, he placed his hand at the back of her neck and gently pulled her closer. He pressed his lips against hers and felt the fire flow between them. It was like the sun rising in his body, the heat and the passion, it was unlike anything he had ever felt before. He placed his other hand at the small of her back, pulled her body closer to his, and pressed his lips more firmly against hers.

Carolyn placed one hand on the back of his neck and the other on his chest. She could feel the speed of his heart increasing and the temperature of his body climbing. Her heart began beating faster as well, within seconds it was beating as fast as his heart. She could feel his strength as he pulled her closer and every inch of her body was tingling with sensation. It was like pins and needles of joy and excitement. Every inch of her was craving every inch of him and she knew he was feeling the same way. Even though she knew that and she wanted him more than anything, she had to stop.

"Wait. We must not continue, Charles." She took a deep breath and took the smallest of steps back.

Charles took a breath as well and looked at her. He was confused and felt a bit lightheaded. "Why?" was the only word he could get out as he sat down on the bed while she stood in front of him.

She smiled at him, caressed the side of his face and explained. "We must not continue because of the task ahead of you. You will need and must have all your wits about you. If we were to continue, you would be distracted and all it would take is a small moment to allow for a mistake that could cost you your entire plan. Then you would not make it back to me, that is, if you wished to make it back to me."

Charles smiled. "I haven't felt a true moment of joy since my daughter was born. I don't know what is happening between us but I do wish to come back to you once this fiasco is done. I just want you to know that this has never happened before with anyone else. I do not go around kissing random women or anything. I do however understand your reasoning and I agree with you. I cannot afford to make a single mistake and now you have given me a reason to make sure I survive the upcoming battle.

Thank you for that Carolyn, it means more to me that you can possibly understand."

Carolyn looked at Charles with a longing to continue what they had just started. "Charles, you are the first and only customer that I have ever kissed or had feelings like this for. For so long I have just focused on my work and nothing else. So, for this to happen, I have no words, only emotions that now belong to you. You must win this battle, you must destroy this monstrous being and you must come back to me." She leaned down and kissed him once more before she returned to mixing her chemicals.

Charles closed his eyes and took a deep breath in. "I must ask you for one last favor. I need a milder sedative to knock out someone who is a vampire but he is also a dear friend. Once I return you will meet him and see that he does not have a corrupt or evil bone in his body. I raised him after his father was murdered in Wills. He fell victim to the monster in my home after my daughter died but he became a vampire in the process of defending himself. He is a good person and will be a great man. I promise you that with unwavering certainty.

"I will do this for you because I know that not every person's heart is filled with rage and hate. I believe that good lives in us all but it's when we choose to do the bad things that our hearts become tainted and corrupt. I am curious though, if this person is your friend then why do you want to make them sleep?" She imagined that he would want all the help he could get.

Charles gave her a little smile, she was truly listening to him. "I made a promise to his father to keep him safe, I already failed him once, I will not fail him a second time. When your mixture puts her in a dream state, I will give him the lesser dose and leave him here safe and out of danger. I will leave him a note and when he awakens he will know I spared him the horror that I will face."

"I could tell you had a kind heart, your soul is tormented by this evil, but once you have defeated this monster you will finally be free." Carolyn handed him two bottles. "The smaller is the diluted one. Give half to your friend and the other half to her, just mix it into a drink and they will be asleep within seconds. The bigger bottle is stronger and must be injected in the vampire every four hours, if you are late on a dose then you have roughly thirty minutes to inject her before it starts to wear off. I added something in there to keep her body paralyzed for a bit after she starts to wake up. Please be very careful and gentle with the bottles, if you break it when you leave I won't be there to make you more." She leaned forward and kissed him once more.

"Thank you Carolyn, I truly appreciate your help. More than that, thank you for giving me something to come back for. I can't say that coming back was a priority until now." He pulled her close, hugged her tight and kissed her. "If its ok, I would like to see you one more time before we depart."

"Charles, as much as I would love that, I don't think it would be wise. You need to be clear headed when you leave, seeing me will only cloud your judgement. I promise, I will be here waiting for your return. Now you must go and make sure that you are fully prepared. This isn't good-bye, it's until we see each other again." She walked him to the door, hand in hand.

"Yes, until we see each other again. Good-bye Carolyn." Charles winked at her as she gently closed the door behind him.

Charles left the saloon and he did so with a new sense of confidence and determination. He stopped at the gunsmith's shop, picked up the ammo and knives he had ordered. He made his way back to the house where Jacob and the others were staying to drop off the ammo and knives. As he brought them in Jacob was looking at him with a peculiar stare.

"Is something wrong Jacob?" He asked with concern in his voice.

"I don't know Charles, you tell me. There is something different about you and I can't quite put my finger on it. Did something happen while you were in town?" Jacob was sure what was different but he had only noticed that presence once before.

Charles tried not to smile. "Nothing bad. I met with the apothecary specialist and she was quite helpful. Very nice woman and very knowledgeable."

"Hmmm, I see. How helpful was she?" Jacob said, implying that something more than a business transaction took place.

"Nothing like that Jacob. She was a very attractive woman but at this time, I cannot afford any distractions.

Our task ahead of us is far too important." Charles tried to avoid making eye contact with Jacob by looking at the ammo.

"I agree that we do have important work ahead of us but something to look forward to, that's never a bad thing. Seems more like it would be proper motivation to complete the task and be sure to make it home safely. I may be young but that's just my opinion." Jacob smiled at his friend.

"I will keep that in mind. Now that we have all the supplies we'll need, I think it is time to find safer lodging. Go tonight, find a place that is unfamiliar to us and store the supplies. John should be back in a few days and we will need to be fully prepared. You, Samuel and Erica will need to have fresh clothes and be sure to get some rest. Everyone needs to be at full strength for this trip and battle. I will see you all soon." Charles was confident that they would be ready at a moment's notice to leave for the ship.

Charles left the house and made his way home. Like always he got washed up and gave his dirty clothes to the house staff. He hid the bottles Carolyn had given him in Chloe's room, a place he knew Cassandra wouldn't go searching. He had the staff prepare dinner and he waited for Cassandra to join him.

She made her way downstairs and joined him at the table. "You look refreshed Charles. Did you have a good day today?"

"I took my horse out riding today, he got a bit rowdy and knocked me off of my saddle. Figured I might as well get cleaned up before dinner, I didn't want to sit here with the day's dirt. It seemed rude to do so." Charles was getting far too good at lying to her, though he knew it was to keep the others safe.

"I do hope you didn't get injured. Horses are such wild things, unpredictable at times. You never know when something so wild will turn on you." She was hinting at something much more than a horse bucking its owner off.

"Cassandra, if I didn't know better, that almost sounded more like a threat than an observation. Is there something you would like to say?" Charles kept his tone even and calm, almost emotionless.

"Not at all, husband. That was simply an observation about wild animals. What reason would I have to threaten you?" She was being coy and was trying to get a rise out of him. Maybe he would slip up, mention Erica and her disappearance.

"How about we just enjoy dinner my love. I had the staff prepare us some delicious steaks, fresh corn and potatoes. Afterwards we can sit by the fire, if that would please you or we could go for a late night ride and enjoy the stars." Charles knew she was playing a game with him but he wouldn't take the bait and lose his temper.

"That does sound absolutely lovely. It's been so long since we've gone on a late night ride. I think that would be a great way to enjoy this fine night." Maybe he is coming around, she thought. Perhaps soon he would finally give in and accept her offer.

They finished their meals and he asked the staff to prepare two horses. They rode away from the house and in the opposite direction of where Jacob and the others were at. He knew of a small lake that wasn't too far from home. As they got there, they could see the stars reflecting off of the lake. They dismounted the horse and walked along the lake after leading the horse to the water to drink. They sat in the grass quietly and just admired the beauty of the night.

Charles heard a rustling in the distance and it drew his attention quickly. "Did you hear that?" He asked with a hint of concern in his voice.

"It's only a rabbit, nothing to fear." Cassandra could hear its heart beating rapidly and she recognized the scent.

"How can you tell?" He asked.

She told him, "I can hear its heart and rabbits have a particular scent to them. I can capture it if you don't believe me."

"I believe you. I guess that all part of your gifts that you have mastered over the years. The ability to hear and stalk your prey from a distance. It must come in handy when you're hunting." He was a bit sarcastic with his words.

"I do not appreciate your tone, but yes it is part of it. I've had many years to practice and strengthen my abilities. If I knew that you wouldn't get angry again, I would offer to show you. But I already know how that conversation goes." She returned his sarcasm.

"I'm glad you know better than to bring that unwanted offer up again. It would be a shame to end the night on a sour note. Wouldn't you agree?" Charles was not enjoying the lake like he should have been and he would be just fine with heading back home.

"I know better? Husband you speak of ending the night sour and yet you provoke me with words like that. Perhaps it would be best if we were to head back, I think the day has made you tired and easily offended." She stood up and went to retrieve the horses.

"Perhaps it has. That fall from the horse seems to be lingering and my aches are getting the better of me." He reached for his horse's reins and patted the horse on the neck.

He offered to help her up onto her horse but she refused. They both got onto their horses and made their way back home in tense silence. They passed the reins off to the staff and went inside.

Charles asked Cassandra. "Will you be joining me for the night my dear or will you be staying up for a while."

"I have slept most of the day already, perhaps I will join shortly. I would like to sit by the fire and enjoy a glass of wine. Goodnight Charles. Sweet dreams." Cassandra had no intention of going to bed just yet. She noticed that they rode away from their usual path. She intended to find out why.

Once Charles was asleep, Cassandra proceeded outside. First she went to the stables to see if there was anyone hiding, she found no one beside some confused stable workers. She bid them goodnight and she continued her search. She noticed a house off in the distance, one she had never noticed before she used her speed and rushed to the house. There was a hint of horse manure which she found odd. The door was locked so with a single hit from her hand the door burst open. She walked in and noticed the house was completely empty. She walked around sniffing the air, hoping to pick up on something. She did but it was only her husband's scent. She found it strange that he was here by himself. Perhaps she would ask him about it or maybe she would use the house to store her next meal.

She ran into town and grabbed a drunken man who had stumbled out of the bar. She grabbed him and dragged him back to the empty house. He screamed and begged for her to let him go. She just stared at him, he fell silent. She grabbed the man by the throat, ripped the flesh from around his neck and engorged herself. The man's corpse collapsed to the floor as he gasped for air. She watched him choke on his own blood before he finally died. She wiped her mouth and licked her fingers clean. She returned home, washed her face off and burned the clothes she was wearing so

Charles would not see the bloodied mess of her dinner. She sat in her chair, enjoyed a glass of wine and started into the fire.

<u>Chapter Eight</u>

John had finally arrived in Savannah to meet with Captain James. He made his way to the captains home and admired the beauty that the city offered. Once he arrived, he walked up to the captain's door, knocked and waited as he heard footsteps coming down the hall.

Captain James opened the door, smiled and extended out his hand to John. "John, my old friend, please come in. It's good to see you. What brings you all the way out to Georgia."

John shook Captain James' hand, with a smile, he followed the captain inside of his home. "It is good to see you James but I'm afraid I'm here by request of Charles. He has tasked me with setting up transportation on the family's ship."

"Ah, business first then we will have a drink. I haven't heard from Charles in quite a while, after Chloe passed I expected him to sell the ship and be done with us.

I'm grateful he didn't, what is it that he is needing from me?" Captain James was eager to find out what Charles was asking of him.

"He has requested transport to an island that is south of Florida and was known to be visited by his parents. The nature of these trips must remain a secret and he is also willing to pay extra for the secrecy. He would also need the use of the guest cabin and secure working positions for two people who are working with him." John was vague with the details he was giving Captain James. He was unsure how much or how little information would be needed to secure what Charles needed.

"Well, I see no problem with getting him to where he needs to go, after all, it is his ship. The crew will do as I tell them, so if he wants to give the men a bonus for their secrecy then they would be happy to accept it. Believe me when I say that they do not turn down money. In regard to the number of trips there, I would only recommend making one trip there and back. For multiple trips it would consist of double the amount of supplies such as food and water. You're hiring two crews, one for each trip and that will not be cheap. Basically, with no offense intended, I would inform him that we will only be making one round trip."

James was uncertain how Charles would take that news but it was the safest plan and being that he was the captain it was his call.

John looked at James for a moment in silence, he was trying to anticipate Charles' reaction to James's decision. "Well, as you said, you are the captain so there is no point in arguing with you. I will add that we will need two crew spots for a cook and an assistant, they are Charles's associates but he wants them below deck for the duration of the voyage. Lastly, some room in the ships hold, for some supplies he is needing to bring along."

James replied. "That's not a common request but I am sure it can be arranged easily. What kind of cargo are we talking about here and how much space will be needed?"

"He did not mention what the cargo was but I am sure it won't take up much space. Are we in agreement?" John asked and reached his hand out.

"I believe we are good sir, now how about we toast to seal the deal." James shook John's hand and stood up to pour two glasses of whiskey.

"Sounds great." Both men clinked their glasses together and drank the whiskey. John also pulled out some of the money Charles had given him and handed half of it to James. "Consider this a down payment from Charles for the upcoming excursion."

"That is awfully considerate of him, please thank him for me. Now how about we head over to the saloon in town for a few drinks, my treat seeing as I just got a payday" James laughed as he smacked John on the back playfully.

"I mean if you insist, who am I to refuse such a generous offer? Lead the way Captain." John laughed as he followed James out of the house and began making his way down the street.

The two men drank for hours, but by the time they left the saloon it was close to three in the morning. James stumbled his way back home after walking John to the train station. John said he wanted to wait at the train station so he could make it back home in decent time. James offered to let him sleep at his home in the spare room but John didn't want to take the chance of missing the train. Once John got comfortable on one of the benches he pulled his hat down over his face and dozed off.

John was startled awake by the abrupt sound of the train's horn blowing as it pulled into the station, the sound was even louder due to the after effects of all the alcohol he had drunk with James. John almost fell to the floor as he tried to get up off of the bench. He had caught himself with one hand on the back of the bench and he was able to get both feet under himself to gain his composure. He boarded the train, sat down and instantly fell back asleep. Even with the sounds of the train and its horn, he did not wake up for several hours.

In fact, by the time he woke up the train was about thirty minutes away from his stop. He adjusted himself in his seat and sat upright. The train station was in the neighboring town, so he stopped at the restaurant next to the general store. He ordered himself a cup of coffee, two scrambled eggs, bacon and a side of toast. He devoured his breakfast quickly and had an additional two cups of coffee. By the time he was done, he was feeling great, all he needed was a shower and he would be right as rain.

He rode straight to the house and saw that Charles was out front and he appeared to be getting ready to head out. He snapped the reins and hurried his horse over to Charles.

"How was your trip John? I do hope you come with some good news for me." Charles said as he shook John outreached hand.

"I do believe it is good news but it is not entirely as you had asked for. I spoke with Capt. James and he has agreed to everything except one thing. He stated that he'd only make one round trip pass to the island. He claimed that the cost for two separate trips was simply not a smart decision, considering that it's twice as much, food and supplies. He stated that he means no offense to you but as the captain he does reserve the right to make changes or set some of the guidelines for the ship and its use." John stood there nervously waiting for Charles to respond.

"Hmm... I see. That is not a favorable decision but I can respect the decision of the captain. This will however make the time table that we are working with a shorter one. I will need to speak to Jacob and Samuel immediately to begin preparations. Now that you are back, I need to ask one last favor of you. I intend to sedate Jacob. I do not want him to be a part of this venture, I know he wants to get revenge on Cassandra especially since she is the one who murdered his father but it is the only thing I can do to protect him. I already failed him once and I refuse to fail him again." Charles said stoically.

"I understand Charles. How do you plan on sedating him and what do I do when he wakes up to find out you left without him?" John was concerned about the fact that Jacob was a vampire and he had no idea how to calm an angry vampire.

"I would definitely keep my distance, perhaps maybe keep a door between him and yourself. Once he's out and I have Cassandra successfully sedated, we can bring him into the house and back in his old room. The doors are pretty solid and it is somewhere familiar to him." Charles was almost positive that that would be enough to help calm Jacob.

"Ok. I will keep him safe until your return, you have my word." John shook Charles's hand in agreement.

"Now that we have that settled, I must go see Jacob and Samuel to update them. I told them to find somewhere else to stay and the place they found is north of town. They will need to be ready and I will need to make sure I have the crate ready to transport Cassandra after she is sedated." Charles had a serious yet nervous look on his face.

"Crate?" Said John.

"Yes, I will need to put her into something to move her around without raising anyone's suspicion. After you left I went to the local carpenter and gave him the exact measurements of a crate to build. It's not too different from a coffin, which is fitting considering it will be the last thing she'll ever sleep in." Charles spoke with a hint of relief in his voice. He was growing tired of having to constantly watch his back around Cassandra and wonder when or if she would attack him. Plus, with meeting Carolyn, he wanted a chance to be happy again.

"That all sounds a bit morbid to me but I am not the one living with that monster. I just hope and pray that you are able to put this nightmare behind you. You are a good man Charles, you don't deserve to deal with this kind of madness." John spoke with remorse in his voice. He had known Charles for a very long time and he never once did anything to warrant living in fear every day.

"Thank you John. I know I have asked a lot of you recently but there is no one I trust more than you to handle these matters." Charles smiled and then mounted his horse. "The day is young my friend, go and enjoy it. I will be seeing you seen enough."

Charles began his ride to go see Jacob and Samuel, as he rode through town he thought about stopping to see Carolyn. He knew she had said that they shouldn't see each other til he returned from the island but every bone in his body ached to see her. He looked up to the windows above the saloon, and as if his prayers were heard, there she was standing in the window. Her beauty shone through the window like the sun peaking over the clouds as it began to rise. He smiled and tipped his hat to her, she smiled and blew him a kiss. He smiled as he continued his ride.

As he approached the house where they were staying he saw someone peeking through the wooden shutters. The front of the house was facing south so he was in a clear line of sight for whomever was peeking through. As he got closer he announced himself, "It's Charles, I'm gonna be coming inside shortly." He dismounted from his horse and walked it to the trough. He walked to the door, knocked and entered.

It was early enough that Jacob and Samuel had not gone to sleep yet. They were sitting in chairs at the table in the kitchen. The windows had been boarded up to keep the light out and away from them. Charles could tell that they were tired and would want to sleep soon.

"I'll try and keep this short and to the point. John has returned from talking to Captain James. He is going to do as we have requested with only one change in the plans. He is only willing to make a single trip there and back. It's not what I wanted but his reasoning makes sense and to be honest, I think it is probably better that way. We will just have the supplies brought to shore first, then we will bring Cassandra ashore and we will end this horrific nightmare once and for all." Charles felt confident with his plan, even with the new adjustments.

"Do you really think we will have enough time to get everything ready to go, get it loaded and do as you say?" Jacob asked. "When will we leave and how are we going to avoid being out in the sun?"

"It's simple." Samuel chimed in. "We will leave before Charles does. The night before we leave the moment the sun goes down. With our speed, we can be there way before the train even comes close to arriving. John and Erica will accompany Charles during the day, while we sleep on the ship. We can hide in the hold of the ship until they arrive, which if timed right should be around dusk." Samuel just sat there as he rattled off the practically perfect plan.

Charles was impressed by how Samuel was able to come up with all that so quickly. "Samuel, how did you do that? To be able to come up with all that so fast and effortlessly, I am in awe."

Samuel just smiled and winked at Charles. "I got ya covered boss."

Charles chuckled to himself. "Ok. Looks like we have our plan. I think we need to get this plan in motion. I do not want to wait anymore, so we will be leaving in two days. Tonight, I will begin adding the sedative to Cassandra's wine, so by tomorrow night when she drinks she will be knocked out. I've had a special crate made to keep her locked in and I will be keeping watch over her till we arrive." Charles was now more serious than he had ever been before.

"We will be ready Charles. I think I speak for everyone here when I say, we are all ready for this nightmare to be over." Jacob spoke with a determination that he tried to use to mask his fear.

Everyone stood up in unison as if they were agreeing with Jacobs sentiment.

"Erica, this is where you will prove that you truly want to earn our trust back and show where your loyalty is. You will be coming with John and me when we transport Cassandra from the house to the train. After that you and I will be riding together with her locked up in the crate. I can only suggest that you do not choose to cross me or try to betray me." The assertive tone in his voice made Erica shudder.

"Yes sir. I made you a promise and I intend to keep it." She was looking at him dead in the eyes and she did not break the line of sight until he began to walk towards the door.

"OK. We all have our jobs to do and we need to be absolutely one hundred percent ready to go. I'm going to head back to the house and start preparing the sedative. The next time we see each other our plan will be in full swing. Get some rest." Charles nodded to them and left the house.

He mounted his horse and started his journey home. As he made his way through town he thought to himself, this was going to be the last time he rode through town until he came back. It was a somber thought and he knew that more than anything he needed to make sure that

Cassandra did not make it back. For his sake, for Jacob's and now for Carolyn.

He snapped the reins on the horse and sped up in order to get home quickly. He wanted to get home and begin mixing the sedative with her wine. Tomorrow he will pick up the crate. He needed to make sure it was completely ready and secure to keep Cassandra contained until they made it to the island. That crate and the sedative would be the only thing keeping him safe during the trip.

As he approached the house he had another thought, this one more intrusive and drastic, he thought about filling the house with gunpowder and just setting it on fire. He would lose everything he owned but he would also take care of his Cassandra problem in the process. He laughed at the idea but knew he couldn't do that. That house has been his parents and it was Chloe's home. Along with all the bad memories, he has so many more good memories that he wanted to hold on to those memories. Even if he didn't make it back, that house would serve as a memorial to the people who died because of Cassandra's reign of terror.

He approached the stable, dismounted from his horse and handed off the reins to the stable workers. He thanked them for all their years of hard work and loyalty to his family. They looked at him with appreciation and with confusion, he had never thanked them like that before. They watched him as he walked to the main house, as he got to the door he looked back and they quickly got back to work.

As usual he got cleaned up, handed off his worn clothes and thought about lunch. He stopped in Chloe's room to get the sedatives and proceeded to his study. He had the kitchen staff bring him up some lunch and a bottle of wine. He didn't tell them what he was planning for the wine because he was unsure if any of them were working with Cassandra. He hoped that Erica had been the only one who gave into Cassandra's evil offer.

When the food and wine finally arrived, Charles thanked the staff and closed the door behind him. He took the bottle over to his dresser where he had a cork screw and the sedatives. He poured just a bit of the bottle of the sedative into the wine bottle and gave it a few swirls to mix it up. He watched as the two chemicals mix together and become one. He re-opened the bottle and took a whiff but only smelled the sweet scent on the wine itself. He sat the bottle down on the dresser and went to sit down in his chair. He leaned back in his chair and fell asleep.

He dreamt that he was in this strange machine, it was moving down a long stretch of grey road with other machines moving next to him. He looked around and saw a young woman sitting next to him, she was quite attractive. He saw a few more people that he had never seen before. He looked out the window and was taken back by what he saw, it was his estate. The house looked old and weathered, it looked abandoned, deserted and forgotten. The grass was overgrown in some places and some areas were bare. The tree where he hid and discovered Jacob was still alive, was knocked over. He watched as he moved past the driveway. He mumbled the words, "I'm Home" and then he woke up. Still sitting in his chair, he looked around the room.

"Such a strange dream." He said out loud as he poured himself a glass of whiskey. He drank down the whiskey, grabbed the bottle of wine and made his way downstairs. Once he got downstairs he added the bottle of wine to the dinner tray that was going to be used for this evening. He sat by the fireplace, waiting, knowing that Cassandra would soon be making her way down the stairs.

As he was sitting there, gazing in the fire, he was startled by a hand touching his shoulder. He looked up and saw it was Cassandra. "You startled me, my love. I did not hear you come downstairs or come up behind me."

"My apologies, husband. I did not mean to frighten you, you seemed to be enjoying the fire and I didn't want to break your concentration. However, if you are ready to eat, dinner is ready." She said with a mischievous smile. She enjoyed the fact that she was able to scare him, even if it was accidental.

"Yes, I am ready for dinner. Thank you for coming to get me. Did you sleep well?" He asked as they made their way to the dinner table.

"Yes I did. It was quite restful and I feel energized. What were you thinking about while you were looking at the fire? You appeared to be pretty far lost in your thoughts." She said with some curiosity.

"I was just thinking about a strange dream I had. I was looking at our home but it was much older looking and it was just strange. I am glad you were able to get some good rest." He sat down across from her at the dining table after moving her chair in for her.

"How was your day, did you do anything exciting?" She asked as she gazed at him from across the table.

"It was an OK day. I made a trip into town to put in an order for some food supplies for the kitchen staff. It was a nice day for a ride to town, it was a warm day." He replied as dinner was placed in front of him.

Charles needed to do his best to keep a calm and normal demeanor with Cassandra. Just the slightest bit of something out of the ordinary could tip her off and being this close to ending this nightmare, he couldn't take any chances. He had to focus on not eating his dinner so quickly, it was like his body was trying to speed everything up and get to tomorrow's dinner. By tomorrow night he would be preparing to take Cassandra to the train to head to the boat and then to the island. It seemed so close but he knew a lot could happen over the next two days and that wasn't counting the time it would take to get there by ship. That was easily another day or two depending on the weather.

"Would you like me to pour you a glass of wine my love?" Charles smiled at Cassandra as he reached for the bottle.

"Thank you darling. Don't forget to pour yourself some of your favorite whiskey, so I won't have to drink alone." She smiled at Charles quite lovingly.

"You read my mind." He said as he poured himself a glass. He smiled and raised his glass. "To our health and the future." He drank a sip of his whiskey and set the glass down. "Would you like to go sit by the fire?"

"Yes, that would be lovely. Perhaps you could kindly refill my glass before we move to the fire." She noticed that she had finished that glass a bit quicker than usual but maybe it was the fact that they had a nice dinner.

"Absolutely." He walked over, grabbed the bottle of wine and poured her another glass. He wondered if the sedative was working because she drank that glass faster than she usually does. He also knew if they sat by the fire she would be more relaxed, allowing the sedatives to work better.

They walked to the living room, Cassandra sat first and Charles handed her the glass of wine he poured for her. He also gave her her blanket that she sometimes put over her legs while she sat there. He then walked over to his chair and sat down after grabbing his glass of whiskey.

"How did you like your dinner?" He was trying to make small talk but he really just wanted to go to bed.

She yawned. "Yes thank you. The staff did an excellent job preparing the food. I must have eaten quite well, I am feeling a bit sleepy."

"I know how you feel, I am kinda tired myself. How about some fresh air, it is a beautiful night." He was seeing how effective the sedative was in such a small dose, though he needed to make sure that tomorrow when she drank the stronger version she stayed asleep until they arrived. He also knew that the sedative would have to be given several times during the journey to the island.

"I think I would enjoy that, I'll bring my blanket so we can sit and look up at the stars." Cassandra said after another but longer yawn.

They stood up and made their way to the backdoor of the house. They walked out about thirty feet from the door, set up the blanket and sat down. Charles was slightly nervous about this idea because he was feeling drained from the day and didn't want to fall asleep out in the backyard, not to mention mere yards away from where they were sitting is where she attacked Jacob.

She could see him staring at the trees and assumed that he was thinking about the incident with Jacob. She still wondered how much he actually knew about her involvement, if he knew at all.

"I can't believe how close we are to where poor Jacob died. It still breaks my heart every time I think about him and realize that he's gone." She could see the reaction on Charles's face. It was one of pain and anger.

"Yes. The very spot where some crazed evil animal tore into an innocent boy's body, stealing his life away from him." He specifically chose those words because it was exactly how he felt about her and her actions.

Annoyed by Charles's words, she replied. "I hardly think we can call an animal who may have very well believed it was protecting itself from something far worse, evil. Perhaps it thought the boy was there to harm its family, steal its loved ones away. If you back an animal into a corner, it has no other choice than to attack." She could feel her annoyance turning into anger.

"So, you would choose to defend an animal that killed someone that was basically like a son to us? Jacob was a part of this family, he was a friend and I made a promise to his father to watch over him. And I failed both of them." Charles was getting angry so he stood up and looked at Cassandra. "I am going inside and going to bed. This conversation is only going to turn into an argument and I do not want that. He knew if he didn't leave now he was going to say something that would either give away what he was planning or possibly anger her enough to do something he wouldn't live to regret.

"Fine, go ahead and leave." She was annoyed that he was so easily willing to walk away from her comments, part of her was waiting for him to admit he knew it was her. Maybe deep down, she thought, it would be a relief to know and see how he truly felt about her. For Cassandra her patience was wearing thin for her husband, soon enough she would take the choice away from him and force him to become like her. She just didn't know when she would do that.

Charles walked away from her angry but proud of himself for not giving in to her attempts to provoke him. He knew that he only had to wait one more day, then she would be trapped and unable to provoke anything from him. He continued inside and went straight to his study. He realized that more often than anything he had been sleeping in there instead of his bedroom, the thought of sharing a bed with Cassandra was no longer feasible to him. All he wanted was to end the nightmare that she had become and then he would sleep peacefully in his own bed. There was also the simple fact that he was terrified of her and did not want to give her any opportunity to turn him into a monster like her. So, he made himself comfortable in his chair and he fell asleep.

Cassandra was still lying on the blanket outside, she was feeling unusually relaxed and at peace. She began to wonder if maybe she was being too hard on Charles, after all he did accept her for what she was and still loved her. She thought to herself, "Was it really necessary for her to do what she did to Jacob?" Had she made a mistake and let her actions ruin something she had never had before. She was beginning to feel more remorseful than she had ever felt and it made her see herself as something bad, perhaps even evil. She began to wonder what would happen if she just sat there as the sun rose. Let the warmth pour over her like a blanket and allow herself to be ended while in that embracing glow. She looked down as a tear rolled down her cheek and fell onto her hand.

"NO!" She said aloud. She would not allow that to happen, she stood up and looked around. She was a strong woman gifted with the powers of the night, she was a hunter and she would not fall prey to the feelings of a wounded man. She would invigorate herself and be that hunter she worked so long to be, she decided she needed to feed. In her mind, no home cooked prepared meal could replace the feel of chasing down your prey. The enjoyment of biting into her meal as their fear made their heart beat faster, with that first bite blood gushing from the wound and gulping down every last ounce as they screamed and begged for someone to come help.

She felt adrenaline coursing through her veins, her body tingled with excitement as she sped off into town and her teeth extending, waiting to be sunk into the flesh of some unprepared victim. She kept to the shadows as she stalked a man who had just walked past the general store. He mounted his horse and began heading west down a dark path. As she followed the stranger, she increased her speed to keep up with the horse. The moment the town was no longer in sight she leapt at him and knocked him off of the horse. The horse began bucking and neighing in fear and then took off into the night. The man stood up and pulled his gun. He moved around, looking in every direction for whatever it was that hit him. Cassandra was perched in a tree just above the man, she growled and the man looked up. Before he could even get a shot off she dropped down from the tree and pinned him to the ground. His gun flew out of his hand and his head bounced off of the hard dirt. He screamed for help as she ripped his head to the side and she sunk her teeth so far into his neck that she hit a vein that spewed blood into her mouth and all over the ground. She drank and drank and finally stopped to take a breath. The man, who was barely alive, tried to turn over to his stomach and crawl away. Cassandra stomped on the center of his lower back breaking his spinal cord. She straddled the man while he was face down in the dirt, sobbing and pleading for his life. She pulled his head back and snapped his neck, there was a loud crunch like a branch being broken into pieces. She moved his head to the side and drank more of the man's blood before dropping his lifeless head onto the dirt.

She licked her lips clean and raced back home. She was covered in the strangers blood. It stained her hands and face, with the bucket from the water well she cleaned off the dried blood. Her dress, which started the night out as a sky blue, was spattered with a deep red and almost purplish tint. She tore it off, once she was inside the house, and threw it into the fireplace. It took a moment for it to catch fire but once it did the smoke rushed out of the chimney as the flames ate the dress leaving only a pile of ashes in its place. She was fully naked as she walked to the bedroom for fresh clothes. She noticed Charles' study door was closed, she tried to turn the knob and it was locked. She ran her clawed finger nails across the door as she continued to the bedroom where she would once again sleep alone.

Chapter Nine

Charles woke up to find deep scratch marks on the outside of his study door. That in itself added more fuel to his already burning hot fire that burned for Cassandra's demise. He knew that today would be the day that all his planning and sacrifices paid off. At dinner he would give her the stronger dose of the sedative and then with the help of Jacob and Samuel get her locked securely into the crate he had made. Then it was a train ride to the ship and off to the island. It all sounded so easy and perfectly planned but nothing ever goes one hundred percent according to plan.

He went down to the kitchen and had breakfast. From there he grabbed the bottle of wine that he had poured the sedative in the night before. Knowing that she enjoyed that bottle, he decided to add the higher dose to it. With what was still remaining in the bottle plus the addition of the greater amount he figured it would give the sedative an added kick. He poured in the sedative and gave it a quick swirl to mix it in.

He decided to take a quick trip into town to get extra clothes for the journey. He couldn't pack clothes he already had due to them being in the room where Cassandra was sleeping. He bought two shirts, two pairs of pants and an extra set of undergarments including socks and underwear. He stuffed them into his riding satchel and placed the bottle the sedative was in securely between the clothes. He figured it would give the bottle some much needed protection and keep it from breaking. Charles stopped at the stable where he had the crate hidden, he walked around it once more inspecting it and making sure there weren't any damaged areas where she could escape if the sedative failed.

Once he completed his inspection, he headed back inside the house. There was still quite a bit of day left before dinner time. He thought maybe he should get some sleep since he was going to be up for a good portion of the night. He went back to his study and made himself comfortable. He sat there thinking, this is going to be the last time I have to sleep in this chair. Very soon he would be able to enjoy the comforts of his own bed and not have to live in fear anymore. Maybe he would be able to have Carolyn come over for dinner and enjoy a truly peaceful evening. With that thought, he fell asleep with a smile on his face.

With what felt like a blink of an eye, he was already waking up. He could see from the window that he slept a fair portion of the day away. He got up and went down to the kitchen. He requested that the staff prepare a special dinner for himself and Cassandra. He had picked up a couple of steaks from the town's butcher and asked them to prepare the steaks with chopped potatoes and corn on the cob. The staff were surprised by his request but they did as he asked of them.

Charles returned to his study to retrieve the bottle of wine with the sedative in it. He carried it downstairs and set it on the dinner tray. He instructed the staff that they were not to touch the wine bottle, he said it was a special bottle that he had purchased especially for Cassandra. They acknowledged his request and went on preparing dinner.

By the time dinner was finished, Cassandra was making her way down the stairs. She glimpsed at him and spoke. "Dinner smells quite delicious tonight. Is there a special occasion I don't know about?" She asked Chuck with curiosity in her voice.

"No special occasion, I just wanted to enjoy a nice dinner with you." Charles said as he poured her a glass of wine.

He walked over to his whiskey cabinet, picked up a new bottle and opened it. He poured himself a glass and walked over to the dining room table and sat down in his usual seat across from Cassandra. The kitchen staff brought out dinner and returned to the kitchen. They both looked at their meals, smiled at each other and started to eat dinner.

"This meal is exquisite darling, thank you." Cassandra was truly enjoying her meal.

"You are welcome, I am glad you're enjoying it." Charles replied. "How about a toast?"

"That would be lovely, what shall we toast to?" She asked.

"To the wonders of the future and good health." Chuck raised his glass and she raised hers, they clinked their glasses together and drank. Chuck watched Cassandra drink her wine as he swallowed down his whiskey.

Cassandra had taken a big gulp of her wine and continued to eat her dinner. She drank down the rest of her wine and set the glass down. She began to feel warm and a bit dizzy. "I think this wine is going straight to my head." She said as she took another bite of her steak.

"Are you feeling ok my love?" Charles asked her, as he waited for the sedative to fully kick in.

"Yes, I am fine. Perhaps some more wine. I think as I eat, the food will balance out the feelings from the wine." She said as she continued to eat.

Charles stood up, picked up the bottle of wine and he poured her another glass. He sat back down and continued eating his dinner. By the time he had finished his dinner, Cassandra was barely able to keep her eyes open. As she took the last sip of wine from her glass, her head tilted back and she collapsed to the floor. He just sat there finishing the last bite he was chewing and walked over to her body. He could visually see the rise and fall of her chest so he knew the sedative was doing its job.

He walked over to the front door and let out a loud whistle, which signaled Jacob and Samuel to bring the crate in. For a normal human the crate would have been quite heavy, but for Jacob and Samuel there was absolutely no problem. Before they placed her in the crate Charles had them tie her hand and feet together. Once that was done, and she was in the crate, they nailed the bottom part of the lid shut. The top portion was on hinges and was secured with a lock that only Charles had a key for. This was done because he would have to administer the sedative to her several times throughout the journey. If he missed even one dose he took the chance that she would wake up and wreak havoc.

They loaded the crate into a wagon that Charles would drive to the train station. Charles asked Jacob and Samuel to join him for a drink after the crate was loaded up, the two men smiled and got to work strapping the crate in place. Charles poured himself and Samuel a glass of whiskey but for Jacob, Charles mixed in the small bottle of sedative that Carolyn had given him. He knew Jacob would be angry with him but it was something he needed to do, the only way to keep the promise he made his father.

Both men came in and joined Charles near the fireplace.

"I want to thank you both for all the work and planning that went into this ordeal. I know we have had to move the time frame up but I wouldn't have been able to do this without either of you." Charles handed them their glasses as he spoke, he was careful to make sure Jacob got the correct one. The three men clinked their glasses together and drank down the whiskey. Jacob stumbled a bit and looked up at Charles, who was watching him intensely.

"What's going on?" He struggled to speak. "What did you do?"

"I am sorry Jacob but I made a promise to your father to keep you safe. I failed once but I will not fail a second time. If I make it back, I hope you can find it in your heart to forgive me." Charles said to Jacob as he caught him before he hit the floor.

"Samuel, please help me carry him up to his room. John will be by tomorrow to check on him and unlock the door." Charles noticed Samuel watching him with confusion. "I know this may seem cruel and strange but Jacob's father and I were very close. We were like brothers and on the day he died he asked me to look out for Jacob and keep him safe. When Cassandra attacked him, I failed him but when I discovered he was still living it was like a second chance to protect him. I hope you can understand why I had to do what I did."

Samuel stepped forward, grabbed Jacobs feet and looked directly at Charles. "Sir, that is a kind and noble thing you have done. You're a good man Charles, I admire your courage and compassion for the boy."

"Thank you." Charles said as they carried Jacob up to his old room. Jacob was set on the bed and Charles locked the door after exiting the room. Both men went out to the wagon where Erica and John were waiting for them. Charles slung his riding satchel over his shoulder and climbed up into the seat. Erica sat between Charles and John as they made their way to the train station.

Once they arrived at the train station Charles went to speak to the train conductor, he was able to secure a private section of a train car. He did that so no one would be suspicious of the large crate that he was transporting. This time it took Samuel, Charles and John to load the crate into the car. Once it was loaded Charles thanked John for his help, handed him the keys to the house and showed him which key unlocked Jacob's door. They shook hands and John left with the wagon.

On the train Charles and Erica sat across from each other but with the crate between them. Charles made sure of this because that way they could each see if anyone was coming from either direction. Charles got comfortable and put his feet up on the crate.

"That seems a bit disrespectful." Erica said.

"Disrespectful to who? The monster locked inside this crate? After all the terror she has caused and lives she has taken, you worry about being disrespectful to her? Why?" Charles was puzzled by Erica's comment.

"It's not that I agree with her decisions or actions but the power she has and the knowledge she has gained of hundreds of years. If she had chosen a different path, a more compassionate and kinder path, she could have been a hero to this world. But she didn't, she was abandoned and forgotten, she became this creature of nightmares. I don't expect you to respect the woman in the box but the fact that she survived all these years is respectable." Erica said all while staring down at the crate.

Charles removed his feet, leaned forward towards the crate and placed his hand on it. "You make a good point but she was given the opportunity to be so much more than a monster. When I met her, I felt nothing but unconditional love for her. When she told me about her secret, I still loved her with all my heart. I accepted what she was because she was the piece that made my heart whole. When Chloe died she blamed herself but I did not, I still loved her because I shared her pain and wanted nothing more than to grieve with my wife. She took that love and broke it when she killed Jacob. She broke it more when I found out that she was the one who murdered Edward, a whole town and even several staff members. Then she burned that love to ashes when she tried to come after me, all because I didn't want to become a vampire like her. She had many opportunities to become something more than a blood thirsty animal, she had a love that accepted her and what she was without asking for anything in return." Charles stopped for a moment, looked at Erica and sighed. "Do you know how to tell when you really truly deeply hate someone?"

"I am assuming it's when they have hurt you and the ones you love?" She was unsure of her answer.

"No. You only hate someone that deeply when you've loved them enough to know what they could've been. Cassandra could have been anything but she chose to be a monster." Charles said to her with a tear in his eye.

He sat back and shifted his gaze out the window. He recalled the dream he had where he was looking out a window at his home as it sat in ruin. He wondered if Jacob would be able to forgive him for leaving him behind and giving him that sedative. So many thoughts raced through his head, he even thought about Carolyn and if he would ever see her again. He had no idea if his plan would be enough to truly and permanently end Cassandra but he had no other choice except to see this through to the end.

The train had been going for about five hours, Charles asked Erica to go check with the conductor and see how much longer until they arrived. She nodded and began heading to the front of the train. Once she was out of sight he began to unlock the crate. He wanted to give Cassandra more of the sedative before they arrived at the ship. He opened the crate, then pulled out the sedative and slightly poured some into her mouth. He tilted her chin up just enough to allow the liquid to slide down her throat. He locked the crate back up and put the sedative safely back into his satchel.

Erica returned and informed Charles that they would be arriving in roughly two hours. He thanked her as she sat back down in her seat. Charles leaned back in his seat, pulled the brim of his hat down and dozed off. Erica remained awake waiting over him and the crate. The train rolled on as she sat in silence. She sat there thinking about what Charles had said to her, "You only hate someone that deeply when you've loved them enough to know what they could've been," his words touched her because she almost became something horrible but he gave her another chance. He allowed her to become something better and she appreciated him for that.

Charles woke up as the train was pulling into the station, after the horn let out its loud whistle, it came to a stop. He instructed Erica to wait with the crate while he went to find somewhere to buy a wagon, two horses and some men to help get the crate from the train car to the wagon. He went to one of the nearby stables and spoke to the owner. After some time, they both came out, shook hands and the owner waived over the stable hands. They were instructed to assist Charles with his cargo and getting to the ship. Once they were done helping him get to the ship and unload the cargo, they were to bring the horses and wagon back.

Charles returned to the train with four men to help load the crate. Erica climbed into the front of the wagon and waited for them to get moving. The crate was loaded up, secured and began its route to the ship. Charles sat in the back with three of the men while Erica rode up front with the driver. Charles could tell that the guys were getting curious about the contents of his crate. "It's a corpse." He said, knowing that the truth was so ridiculous that it made a good joke. The three men sitting around him looked at him with disbelief. Charles started laughing and they did so as well. "It's just some old family junk, dropping it off with a relative who was interested in it." He could see them sigh in relief and he smiled.

They approached the docks where Charles would meet up with Capt. James. He hoped that Samuel was already on the ship and keeping safe below deck. They approached the ship, Charles could see that the crew was already working on getting supplies on board. He instructed the driver to pull as close as he could to the ship as he safely could. Charles got out and greeted Captain James, who was making his way over to him.

"Captain James, it's been a long time, how are you doing?" Charles said as he shook the captain's hand.

"Doing well my friend. It's good to see you, you're looking well. I am surprised your wife isn't here with you. I guess she must be awful trusting to let you out by yourself." He joked. The two men had known each other for some time and always liked to joke crudely.

Charles smiled for a moment and let his reaction turn sorrowful. "Sadly, she passed recently, she fell to a terrible illness. This trip is in her honor, she always wanted to see the ocean and go on an adventure."

Capt. James looked at him puzzled. "I am now afraid to ask what is in your crate. If it's what I think it is and I mean no disrespect, but I truly hope there won't be any odors or strange happenings during the voyage."

"No disrespect taken Captain. There will not be any problems on my end, you have my word." Charles said.

"Sounds good. Let's get your umm… cargo loaded and get on our way." Captain James said with a hint of hesitation in his voice.

Charles had the four men carry the crate from the wagon to the guest cabin on the ship. It was placed opposite of the bed and secured against the wall. Erica had a small cot near the foot end of the crate. Charles thought it was only fair that she be allowed to stay there considering the sleeping quarters for the crew were all men. Charles thanked them for their help and they left the ship to return home. Charles made his way to the galley looking for Samuel, thankfully he found puttering away supplies.

"Ah good, you made it. The captain hadn't mentioned that you arrived so I needed to be sure that you did." Charles said feeling a bit of relief.

Samuel smiled. "Don't worry my friend, this will be a smooth voyage and you will be back home before you know it."

Charles knocked on the ceiling of the galley. "For luck, I don't want to jinx us before we even begin. Hope you're a good cook, otherwise the crew might just throw you overboard." He joked hoping to ease his own nerves.

"Not to worry, I am a damn good cook. In fact, I can cook so well that I can convince the crew to make you walk the plank." Samuel said laughing.

Charles laughed as he made his way back to the cabin. He asked Erica to go and help Samuel with putting away supplies, which she did quickly. After she left, Charles gave Cassandra another dose of the sedative. She didn't even move the slightest bit, with the exception of her chest rising and falling, she really did look like a corpse. A beautiful, deadly and monstrous corpse, one that could tear people to shred and give a kind smile at the same time.

He quickly closed and locked the lid and he made his way to the deck of the ship. Captain James was doing a last round of checks before the ship would set sail to the island. Charles walked over to the Captain and stood next to him as he barked orders to the crew.

"Captain, how long do you think this voyage will take?" Charles asked with some concern and curiosity.

Captain James looked at Charles silently, He was trying to come up with a realistic time frame for him. "Given proper winds and us able to maintain a constant speed, I would estimate three days to a week. Now if we are unfortunate and lose our winds, it could take possibly close to two weeks."

With a look of surprise and shock Charles stared at the captain for a moment. "Two weeks? I do hope and pray we can make it there in less time than that."

The captain noticed Charles's nervousness. "Well, my friend, I think you will be in luck. From the looks of the skies, there may be a storm rolling in sometime after we leave. The winds from that storm should keep us within a three to four day window. I simply mention the longer time frame just to be honest with you and keep you aware of potential possibilities.”

A bit of relief escaped Charles as he looked out to the sea. “That makes me feel a bit better, thank you. One another note, I have brought a gift of sorts for the crew along with the extra payment that I asked John to mention.”

“The crew will be quite pleased with both the bonus and whatever gift you have brought for them. Though, as I told John, it isn’t necessary but greatly appreciated by all.” The captain said. “Will one of your associates bring the gift to the galley or should I have one of my crew retrieve it.”

“It will be brought up and served with dinner, I will have Samuel bring it up and make it available for everyone.” Charles said while making his way to the galley to speak to Samuel.

“Very well. See you at dinner my friend.” The captain said while Charles left the deck. Captain James made his way to the bridge to begin their voyage. “All right men, Heave and a-weigh” He yelled to the crew. They all cheered as they raised the anchor. “Set the sail men and let's get moving. Fair winds and following seas." Captain James yelled.

The ship began moving and making its way further out to sea. Charles felt the ship jerk as the sails caught the winds and started them on their journey. The nerves in the pit of his stomach began to tighten because now there was no turning back, the bulk of his plans had been played out and now it was the final descent. With Cassandra sleeping heavily and secured in his cabin, he made his way to the small bed where he was going to be sleeping. Erica was still assisting Samuel with the supply room so he decided that he would take the opportunity to take a quick nap.

"Do you think everything will go as Charles planned?" Erica asked Samuel.

"I have no doubts that Charles has carefully planned out this entire voyage and will keep the beast deep in its sleep. Once we get to that island, it should be a quick affair and then we will be on our way back home. Safe and sound." Samuel spoke with confidence and certainty.

"How is it that you can be so certain that everything will work out as it is supposed to? Are you not afraid that we can possibly fail or she will wake up either on the ship or on the island and kill us all?" Erica asked him. She was looking for comfort and wished she could share in his optimism.

"Erica, you can either be positive and look to the good things in life or you can dwell on the negative and live in constant fear of what may or may not happen. I choose to be positive and to believe that Charles has everything under control. The moment I choose to believe otherwise, my mind will create so many unlikely scenarios and it will drive me crazy. And if you are wondering, yes I am speaking from experience." Samuel had stopped what he was doing to give Erica his full undivided attention.

She looked at him and smiled. "Thank you Samuel. You have helped me put my mind at ease." She said as they finished stocking the supply room and began preparations for dinner.

Charles had begun dreaming about Chloe again. Except this time, it was when she was born. He was standing there with Cassandra, she had just gone through a grueling labor and delivery of their baby girl. He held Chloe in his arms as she slept, she was wrapped in a warm blanket and he just stood there staring at her. He felt so much love for his sweet tiny Chloe, more love than he had ever felt for anyone in his whole life. He pulled her close to his chest giving her a gentle hug as a tear rolled down his face. As he pulled her away from his chest the room began to darken. He looked around the room, puzzled as to why the lights had gone dim. He looked at Cassandra and she was no longer lying in the bed but now standing in front of him, looming over him with a menacing look on her face. She snatched Chloe from his arms and lifted him off the ground by his throat. She began to tighten her grip around his neck, choking the life out of him. He tried his best to pry her hand off of his neck but he could not. Suddenly he felt a sharp stabbing pain and realized her nails were growing and digging into his neck. She closed her hand, ripping the flesh off of his neck and he dropped to the ground. Blood flowed from his neck like a river flowing through the forest. As he laid there gasping and bleeding, she knelt down next to him and began feeding Chloe the blood from his neck. As he gasped one last time, fully expecting to enter whatever afterlife awaited him, he woke up gasping for air and grabbing his neck.

He looked over and saw Erica sitting on her cot near the crate. He sat up in his bed and placed his feet on the floor to try and reorient himself to reality. "What are you doing here Erica? Shouldn't you be helping Samuel?" He asked her while taking a few deep breaths to calm himself down.

"I was but he finished stocking and dinner is almost ready. He told me to go and get some rest before it was time to serve the crew. I came in her and you were sleeping and you began making some odd noises. I was going to wake you but I was afraid that you might lash out at me. Are you ok? Did you have a nightmare?" She asked him with concern in her voice.

"Yes, I am fine. Thank you for asking. I had a very vivid and disturbing dream, but it is over and I am ready for dinner. Please go to the hold of the ship where our supplies are and grab the box label "crews gift". I will be along shortly." Charles said while getting up from his bed.

Erica did as she was asked and went down to the hold. Charles once again gave Cassandra a dose of the sedative and locked the crate back up. He went down to the dining area in the galley and opened the box Erica had brought up.

"Hello everyone. Some of you may not know me but my name is Charles. I want to thank you all for your hard work and years of dedication to my family while aboard this ship. As a token of my appreciation, I have brought along a case of my favorite whiskey for you all to share and enjoy." The crew cheered and clapped as Charles began passing around the bottles of whiskey.

Captain James spoke up next. "Thank you to our very generous friend here but I would like to add that I expect you all to drink in moderation as we are still working here. Do not make fools of yourselves or fall overboard because I will leave you drunk asses for the sharks." Said the Captain as he grabbed a bottle of whiskey and poured himself a glass.

The crew laughed and acknowledged the captain's orders. Samuel and Erica began to bring plates out for everyone and did so until every crew member had a one in front of them. Then they brought themselves a plate and sat down near Charles. He poured them both a glass of the whiskey and one for himself. They cheersed, took a sip of the whiskey and began eating. Charles looked over at Samuel after his first bite, he smiled and nodded to him.

After dinner was finished, the crew left the galley and went back to their assigned jobs. Some went to the deck of the ship, some went to bed to get some sleep before their shifts, and Samuel and Erica cleaned the dishes. Once done Samuel went up to the deck to get some fresh air and Erica went to the cabin to get some sleep. Charles went up to the deck to speak to Samuel.

"So how long before you have them make me walk the plank?" He joked. "You truly have a gift in the kitchen Samuel, dinner was very good."

"You're too kind Charles. I am simply doing my job, plus a crew full of hungry seamen is a dangerous thing. It's best to keep their bellies full and moods in good spirits. As far as walking the plank, I haven't decided yet." He laughed as he looked up at the sky. "I forget how beautiful the sky is when you are at sea. It's like the sky and seas stretch out forever and meet far off into the distance, gently touching each other like lost lovers kissing." Samuel was enjoying himself and the view that lay out in front of him.

"I didn't know you were such a romantic Samuel." Charles said as he admired the view that Samuel had described.

Samuel looked at Charles and laughed. "There is a lot about me that you don't know my friend. But a love for the sea is something I am happy to share. You should get some rest, there is a storm coming and will be here by the early morning." He said to Charles as he pointed to the lightning that was off in the distance. "We will be heading right through the heart of that storm so you will need your strength to keep that crate safe and secure."

"You're right, I can feel the wind starting to pick up already. Hopefully it works in our favor and gets us to our destination in a timely and safe manner." Charles said as he turned to head to his cabin. Before he left he handed Samuel a half drank bottle of whiskey.

Charles arrived at the cabin to find Erica fast asleep in her cot. He went over to his bed and laid down to get some sleep as Samuel had suggested. Soon that storm would be upon them, this was the prelude to the storm that he would face on the island when they arrived. While he laid there he could feel the ship's speed increasing with the winds from the storm. In the distance Charles could hear the booms of thunder. As they drew closer to the storm, he began to feel the vibrations from the booms. They became more frequent and stronger as they got closer. The booms seemed to comfort him as he began to fall asleep.

He was abruptly awoken but Erica's scream and a thud. He shot and looked over to find her on her knee on the floor. He then felt the sway of the ship as each wave crashed into the hull. He must have been sleeping for a bit because he could see light through the windows of the cabin. Charles quickly went over to the crate and checked it to make sure it was secure. He asked Erica if she knew the time and she replied it should be close to breakfast, as she stumbled her way to the galley. Charles knew Erica was to prepare breakfast so that Samuel could get some rest. He was unsure where Samuel had chosen to sleep but he assumed it was in the hold somewhere far from the light of day.

Charles made his way up to the deck holding on to the walls and rails as waves slammed into the ship more and more frequently. As he got up to the bridge he saw Captain James at the wheel, he was fighting each wave and holding strong. Charles asked him if there was anything he needed him to help with and the captain replied in loud yell. "No, just don't fall overboard. This water will swallow you and you'll never be found."

Charles stood there watching the ship battle the sea for survival. The waves would either crash into the ship or lift it up high and drop them on the other side of the wave. Then all of a sudden, as quickly as the storm started, it slowed down. The waves began to lull and the rain lightened up. Thankfully the winds had not stopped so they kept a good speed and continued forward to their destination.

Captain James relinquished the wheel to his first mate and instructed him to keep the course steady. He went over to Charles smiling. "Well luck must truly be on our side. That storm pushed us forward faster than it should have, which is a bit surprising."

"Surprising how?" Charles asked him.

"Well, a storm like that could have thrown us off course or caused us to drop anchor. Somehow those waves acted like hands and kept pushing us forward in the direction we wanted to go. So, once we can determine our current location, which we will need the stars' help to determine, I can give you a more accurate time frame for our arrival." Captain James said with much confidence.

"Sounds good to me, Captain. I believe Erica should have breakfast ready for those who wish to eat. I will head down there myself shortly." Charles said to the captain while he was looking through his spyglass trying to determine their location.

"Wait." The captain shouted to Charles. "I don't believe this but we are nearing the Keys. The Florida Keys, I can make them out in the distance with my glass here. My god, I have never made that kind of time before." He looked over at Charles in disbelief and joy.

"That must have been one hell of a storm we hit. If you can see the Keys already, with your glass there, what would you say our estimated time frame looks like?" Charles was filled with anticipation and dread while waiting for the captain's answer.

"Given our location and the constant wind speed, I would say that we can potentially be there late tonight. Let me speak with my first mate to confirm this but I believe this to be accurate." The captain hurried over to the first mate and handed him the glass.

As they spoke Charles made his way to his cabin to give Cassandra another dose of the sedative. He then proceeded to the galley where Erica was serving breakfast to the crew. She set down a plate in front of Charles and began to head back to the kitchen when he called her back over.

"Do you know where Samuel is sleeping?" He whispered to her.

"Yes sir, I do." She responded to him.

"Ok. According to the Captain we may reach our destination late tonight. If that is the case then this nightmare may be over sooner than we had hoped. When he awakens please give him this information." Charles said to her while eating his breakfast quickly.

"OK. I will tell him as soon as I see him. Is there anything else you need me to do, Charles?" Erica asked him.

"No, that is all for the moment. Thank you Erica, you have surely proven that you can in fact be trusted and I wanted you to know that." Charles said, smiling at her.

"Thank you Charles. That means a lot to me and I promise that I will continue to earn that trust and keep it." She said to him tearfully.

She continued to the back of the galley to begin washing the dishes and start getting lunch together as Samuel had instructed her to do before she went to bed. She was smiling the entire time while she was cleaning up and preparing the ingredients for lunch.

Charles went back up to the deck to find the captain and the first mate. Captain James was no longer up there so he went over to the first mate to ask about their location and if the captain's estimate was true. The first mate nodded and confirmed that by late tonight they would be arriving at the island that Charles wished to visit. Charles had thanked him and proceeded to his cabin.

Charles was now filled with an urgent suspense and anxiousness. He wanted the time to pass faster so that he could hear the words that meant it was time to proceed further with this journey. He did the only thing he could think of and laid down to sleep. He would wake up from time to time, one of the times he was woken up by Erica telling him she brought him lunch. He fell back asleep leaving the plate on the table nearby. When he woke up next, he ate lunch and gave Cassandra another dose of sedative. He went back to sleep until it was dinner time. Samuel came to wake him this time.

"Charles, come have dinner with the crew. You have been sleeping all day, you need to move around and get some food in your belly." Samuel told him.

"Yes, ok. I will be there shortly, Samuel. Thank you." Charles said to him as he closed the door. Charles gave Cassandra another dose of the sedative and made his way to have dinner with everyone.

It was another delicious dinner that consisted of some beef, bread and a stew. Samuel was indeed an amazing cook and the crew had no problems telling him that much. After dinner Charles went up to the deck and looked out at the water. In the moonlight, he could see the crew busy cleaning the deck, securing lines and some just gathered laughing and drinking the whiskey he provided. Please with what he saw he went back to his cabin and slept a bit more.

Charles was awakened by bells ringing and the words he had been waiting to hear all day. "Land Ho!!!" He jumped up and out of bed so fast that he fell to the floor. He got up and rushed to the deck to see their approach to the island. Samuel and Erica were already up there waiting for him to join them. Charles stepped next to them and stared out at the large land mass that would be Cassandra's final resting place.

Charles rushed to his cabin to give Cassandra what he hoped would be her final dose of the sedative. He locked the crate up and began getting ready to have the crate moved on to a small boat that would take him to the island. Erica and Samuel met him in the cabin to find out what he needed them to do.

"Samuel, can you get a few of the other crewmen to come assist you with getting the crate loaded onto one of the dinghies. Once they have it loaded please come and get me." Charles instructed him as he hurried off to grab some help.

"Erica, can you please have some of the other men start loading our other supplies onto the second dinghy. Once it's loaded up, ride with them and have them unload it near the cave closest to the beach." He needed the supplies and weapons off the ship and ready to use once they got the crate to the cave.

Erica left to get the crew so she could get the supplies to the shore. She was able to get two men to help her load up a dinghy and they began rowing towards land. They had her hold a lantern at the front of the boat so they could see where they were going. She informed them that they were to go towards the cave once they landed ashore. Thankfully there were only a few things to carry to the cave, one crate with the guns and ammo, the second crate contained the bottles with the holy water and garlic mixed together. The last one had the knives and several stakes that Samuel and Jacob prepared.

After they set the crates down they headed back to the beach. They had lit some torches so that the other dinghy could see where they were heading and meet at the same place.

Samuel and the other crewmen loaded the crate into the dinghy. Once loaded they climbed into the small boat and slowly lowered it down into the water. They began making their way towards the shore, rowing slowly and carefully. When they approached the shore the men jumped out and guided the small boat onto the sand. Samuel and the three crewmen carried the crate out of the boat to the sand and set it down so they could get a better handle on it.

The men from the first boat had brought some logs over and made a sitting area around a camp fire that they had started. They sat there with Erica while Samuel and the others carried the large crate to the cave. The fire was roaring while they sat around it laughing and telling stories about pirates on the open seas.

Charles, with a burning torch in hand, guided Samuel and the men to the cave. When they were outside of the cave Charles could feel an unnatural tension in the air. He looked back as the men stood there looking to him for further instructions. He stepped into the cave and asked them to set the crate inside near a smaller cavern. They did as he had instructed and set the crate down a couple of feet away from the cavern entrance. He thanked the men for their help, then told them to gather the other men and return to the ship. He asked one of them to inform the captain that they would return to the ship in the second dinghy once they were done.

Once the men were on the dinghy and safely on their way back to the ship, Charles began to open the supply crates. He grabbed out one of the pistols, loaded it and put it in his belt holster. He loaded a second pistol and handed it to Erica, he went to load a third gun and Samuel refused it.

"I don't need a gun plus with the silver plating, it won't do me any good." Samuel said.

Charles had slid one of the silver bladed knives into the side of his boot. He placed several stakes near the opening of the cavern and moved the smaller crates over to the side of the cave. He looked over at Samuel and Erica, nodded to them and stood up.

"OK, this is it. All of our hard work and planning have come down to these last few moments. Samuel, come help me move her body into the cavern." Said Charles with a hint of fear and nervousness in his voice.

Samuel stepped up to the foot of the crate and Charles stood at the head of it. They both reached in and lifted Cassandra's body up and out of the crate. They cautiously moved into the cavern and set her down on the ground. Her hands and feet were still tied together but if she were to somehow wake up that wouldn't be enough to hold her. Samuel exited the cavern and walked towards the entrance of the cave, looking out at the sky.

Charles still in the cavern picked up one of the wooden stakes, stood over her body and paused for a moment. "I would pray for God to have mercy on your soul but I'm sure the devil will have it much sooner than he will." He knelt down to one knee and placed the stake over her heart. As he was about to plunge the stake down, he heard a strange noise behind him.

He looked back and to his utter horror Samuel had attacked Erica. He had come up behind her, wrapped his arm around her shoulders and sunk his teeth into her neck. When he moved his arm from around her neck, he purposely cut himself and ran his bleeding arm across her mouth. Her body fell to the ground with a hard thud on impact.

"Oh Charles, you are far too trusting and naive. Did you really think it was just a coincidence that there was another vampire in such a close range to Cassandra? You damned fool. Cassandra turned me in Wills, after she killed everyone in that town. She found me and offered me a gift, one that you have foolishly and repeatedly refused. She was well aware of your little plan and that Jacob was still alive. However, you dosing him and keeping him behind was a move that not even I could predict. He will be taken care of after you're dead and we take over the crew of that ship." Samuel was walking towards Charles as he stood over Cassandra's body.

"Why come all this way and wait so long if the plan was just to kill me and Jacob. I may have been naive but that's just stupid." Charles was appalled at Samuel's betrayal but he could see that Erica was moving towards Samuel with something in her hand.

Erica had snuck a bottle of holy water into her pocket. When she and the crew unloaded the crates into the cave, she opened the crate and hid the bottle. Now, on the verge of becoming something monstrous, she chose to fight with the man who had given her the chance to be something more than an evil woman's puppet. She smashed the bottle on the back of Samuel's head, she screamed in pain as the glass cut into her skin and the holy water burned everywhere it landed.

Charles quickly unholstered his gun and unloaded all six silver bullets into Samuel's chest. Samuel, screaming in pain, slammed to the ground and began clawing at his chest. Charles saw Erica glimpse outside and look back at him with tears in her eyes. Charles could see the glow of the sun beginning to rise. Erica grabbed Samuel by the shoulders of his shirt and began dragging him to the cave's entrance. Charles ran over to help her but was met with Samuels boots hitting his chest.

Charles flew into the wall of the cave and hit it so hard that the wind was knocked right out of him. He lay there for a moment, clutching his rib cage and trying to breath. When he finally found his wind he gasped, swallowing air and then coughed so hard that he spit out blood.

Erica had forgotten that she still had the pistol that Charles handed her. The sting of the silver on her lower back was the painful reminder that she needed. She grabbed the gun and aimed it at Samuel's face.

"You think you have the stones to pull that trigger little girl? I don't thi…." Samuels words were cut off by the sound of the gun shot and the impact of the bullet tearing through his mouth. Blood gushed out of his mouth as well as the back of his head. His jaw had shattered and was hanging off the front of his face.

Erica charged at Samuel and grabbed him in a big bear hug. She looked over at Charles, who was making his way back to his feet. "Thank you Charles. If I had to choose someone to be my father, I would have chosen you." She lifted Samuel up off of the ground, dragging him outside of the cave and into the light of the rising sun.

"Erica, NO!!!" Charles yelled out in pain.

The moment the sun touched their skin, smoke began to rise. Erica, screaming in agony, did not stop dragging Samuel. They both burst into flames and screamed out in pain. Erica collapsed with Samuel onto the sand while the sun continued to feed the flames.

Charles was still in pain, from both losing Erica and getting kicked into the cave wall. He cradled his ribs as he made his way back over to Cassandra's body. Twice he almost fell over in pain but he would not let Erica's sacrifice be for nothing. He picked up his stake, he raised it up over his and with every bit of strength he could find he drove it into her heart. He could feel the stake piercing her flesh, pushing through her rib cage and plunging into her cold dead heart. Her eyes shot open and looked directly into his while he continued to push the wooden stake until he felt it hit the ground beneath her.

Blood shot out of her like a geyser, her body began to convulse and smoke. Then as Charles began moving away from her, her skin burst into flames. Charles ran out of the cave as fast as he could, he noticed the large crate had caught fire and he was glad it did. He had left the crates there in the cave as he ran for the dinghy, he climbed into the dinghy and began rowing towards the ship.

As he approached the ship he waved to get the crew's attention. The crew members began shouting and calling for the captain. Two of the crewmen jumped into the water and swam over to Charles. Once he was aboard the ship he collapsed and hit the deck.

Over the next two days he was in and out of consciousness. By the time the ship docked he was finally able to stay awake. Charles thanked the captain and the crew.

"Someday you will have to explain to me what happened on that beach Charles." Said Captain James.

Charles replied to him. "Someday I will but today is not that day. Good bye my friend. Take care of yourself." Charles shook his hand and began making his way to the train station.

He slept the entire train ride, he had no dreams but he was feeling the exhaustion of the journey still. As the train pulled into the station, Charles was met by John.

"It's good to see you, John. How is everything at home? I hope Jacob wasn't too angry with me?" Charles said with some concern.

"It's good to see you as well, Charles. Home is good, getting back to normal I suppose. Jacob was quite angry with you, he has been staying in the house that they found north of town. Shall we head home?” John asked, happy to see that Charles had returned. “By the way, where are Erica and Samuel?”

“That is a story for another day John. Today there is someone I need to go see. You go on ahead home, I will see you later.” Charles said with a smile.

Charles climbed onto his horse. It took him two tries and both times his sides ached more and more. He headed over to the house where Jacob was supposed to be staying. Charles knocked on the door several times but got no answer. “Jacob, I know you're angry with me but I would just like to say that you will never have to worry about Cassandra ever again. It is done and you are safe my son. If you can forgive me, come over for dinner at eight tonight.”

Charles made his way over to the saloon and slowly got off of his horse wincing in pain. He went in and went up the stairs gingerly. He walked over to Carolyn's door and knocked three times. He could hear her yelling “I don’t have any appointments today, come back next week.” He knocked again.

"Are you hard of hearing or can you not follow directions? I said.." She stopped and smiled at him. She pulled him into the room and gave him the biggest hug. She let go when she heard him groan in pain. "What happened? Are you ok?"

"Hello to you too." He laughed. "I am ok, just a bit sore from the journey. I've missed you." He said as he pulled her in closer for a kiss.

Carolyn smiled. "I have missed you too." She said as she pulled him over to the bed.

They began kissing softly at first but the kisses became longer and deeper. She unbuttoned his shirt and gasped, his entire midsection was covered in a mix of deep purple, yellow and brown bruising. She gently kissed his rib cage, his back and made her way up to his neck. He turned around kissing her lips, her neck line and the top of her right shoulder.

This time there were no interruptions, no monsters to kill and no rushing. They finally shared the moment their bodies were aching for, the moment their souls craved for and the moment that their hearts beat for. Afterwards they laid there with her head resting on his chest. They savored the moment and Charles was finally free to be happy.

"Not to kill the mood but there are a few things I need to do today. With my previous situation now handled, there is someone I need to check on. Why don't you come by for dinner tonight at eight?" Charles loved the thought of spending more time with her but he could feel something was off inside of him. Maybe he was just exhausted from the journey, he wasn't sure.

"I would love that, I look forward to having dinner with you later. And maybe some dessert." She winked at him as he got up to get dressed. As he started putting his clothes back on Carolyn thought she noticed something odd with his bruising. She couldn't quite make it out because he was moving around too much.

Charles leaned over and kissed her. He smiled and kissed her again. "I can't wait to see you later, I miss you already." He said as he walked out of the door.

Charles made his way back home. He asked all the staff to meet him in the kitchen. Once there he apologized to them for everything that happened while Cassandra was there and assured them that they will never need to live in fear of her ever again. The staff cheered and clapped, some even shook his hand and hugged him. He asked the kitchen staff to please prepare a big meal for dinner, they smiled and began working. Charles was indeed having a great day.

He walked over to his whiskey decanter and poured himself a glass. He sipped on it as he walked to his study. He sat down in his chair and finally felt at peace. He drank down the last of the whiskey in his glass, he closed his eyes and drifted off

Jacob arrived at the house at seven thirty. He had climbed in through the window in his room. He wasn't sure if Charles wanted the rest of the people in the house to see him just yet. Jacob crept down the hallway to Charles's study. As he entered the room he noticed something strange about Charles, it was a peaceful look on his face. Jacob fell to his knees because he knew why, he was gone.

Just then Jacob heard a female voice calling for Charles, he could tell she was making her way closer to the study. The woman gasped as she entered the room.

"My apologies dear boy, you startled me. You must be Jacob, it's a pleasure to meet you. I'm Carolyn." Carolyn said, smiling until she looked at Charles.

"You know who I am?" He asked, confused since he had no idea who she was.

"Yes, Charles told me about you." Carolyn moved closer to Charles. "He's gone, isn't he?" She asked with tears rolling down her face.

"Yes. He is gone." Jacob said as he shared tears of sadness with Carolyn.

"He asked us both to be here at eight o'clock for dinner. I think he knew he was going to go tonight and he wanted us to meet so we wouldn't have to grieve alone. Good-bye my sweet Charles." She said as kissed him on the forehead.

Epilogue

Jacob

Jacob woke up in his old room, inside of the main house. He walked over to the door to exit out of the room, his irritation increased when he realized the door was locked. He knocked on the door calling for Charles but got no response. His anger was rising and his gentle knock turned into hard, loud banging. He cursed out at Charles for locking him in the room and leaving him behind. He pounded heavily on the door once more but stopped when he heard the key being inserted and unlocking the door.

There was a brief moment of silence before John began speaking to Jacob. "Jacob, it's me John. I am going to open the door but please try your best to remain calm and not do anything rash." He said to Jacob through the door.

"My irritation is not with you, John. It is with Charles, the person who left me behind and denied me my revenge. Revenge for my father and for myself." Jacob said to John angrily.

"I understand your frustration Jacob, I am going to open the door and I would like to speak to you." John said nervously. He slowly opened the door and stepped back so Jacob could exit the room.

"Don't worry John, I have no intentions of harming you. Should we talk in the sitting room by the fireplace?" Jacob said as he made his way to the stairs.

"Yeah, that sounds good to me. I can definitely use a drink as well." John said as he smiled at Jacob.

"Hopefully there isn't any more of that sedative in the bottle that Charles used to knock me out." Jacob said as he chuckled and shook his head.

They went down to the sitting room and John poured himself and Jacob a glass of Charles's whiskey. Jacob looked at the glass suspiciously before taking a sip.

Jacob moved over to the fireplace, added some logs to the fire and lit the fire. John drank his glass down quickly and poured himself another. Both men sat down in the chairs in the sitting room, fully enjoying the warmth as it washed over them like a blanket. Jacob glanced over at John, looking for him to begin whatever conversation he intended to have.

"Jacob, I know that you are upset with Charles and I understand your reasoning. What you need to know is that he did what he did because he felt that he owed it to your father to keep you safe. He told me that he failed Edward once when Cassandra attacked you and he thought you had died. He could not bear for something else to happen to you and he failed your father twice. So, he made sure that you were in the safest place possible, far away from Cassandra. He had no idea if he was going to return but he wanted me to make sure that you knew that. He cared for you as a son." John said as he took another sip of his whiskey.

"Thank you John for that. I understand why he did it, I may just need some time to forgive him for leaving me behind." Jacob said as he stood up and walked over to the fireplace. He gazed into the fire and wondered how Charles's journey was progressing. He wondered if they would be successful or if he would fall to Cassandra's savagery. As he knew, Cassandra was incredibly strong and quite ferocious.

"What will you do now Jacob? Do you plan on staying here at the estate? Charles requested that I ensure you have everything you could possibly need." He did to Jacob as he finished his drink.

Jacob smiled. "Of course he did, but I can't stay in this house. There are too many bad memories here and they haunt me every second that I'm here. I saw a small house that was abandoned just north of the town. I'd like to make it my home, if you wouldn't mind helping me with that." Jacob said to John with hope in his eyes. It was the first time he had felt hopeful in a very long time.

"Absolutely. First thing in the morning I will head down to the sheriff's office and make sure that whatever paperwork is needed will be filled out with no issues. Whatever else you need for it, I will make sure you have or have the means to purchase it." John stood up and walked over to Jacob and extended his hand.

Jacob shook John's hand and made his way to the front door. "I think I will enjoy the night. It has been too long since I was able to go out without having to worry about being seen or discovered by Cassandra." Jacob said, smiling as he walked over to the door. He exited the house and took in a big breath of night air. He then exhaled with relief and a new found feeling of joy. He made his way into town and just casually walked around. He stopped in front of the saloon and decided to head in for a drink. As he entered, he immediately noticed a scent that reminded him of Charles. Jacob looked around the saloon but obviously did not see him, he did see a woman sitting by herself with a look of worry and distress. There was something peculiar about her but he decided to just mind his own business and sat at the bar.

"What can I get ya?" The bartender asked him.

"Just a shot of whiskey." He replied.

The bartender poured the drink and set it down in front of Jacob. He picked up the glass and drank down the alcohol. He looked at the glass for a moment, then set it down and nodded to the bartender for another. He drank that one down and paid his tab. He got up, making his way to the exit, he looked back at the woman who was still sitting at the table alone. He nodded to her and she politely smiled at him. He walked out of the saloon and went over to the house that he had been telling John about. He quietly looked around the house to make sure it was truly abandoned.

He checked the front door but it was locked. He went around back and the back door was unlocked. He went in and looked around. There was spoiled food on the table and everything else was covered in dust. He threw the food out back, figuring some animal would make a meal out of the food. He began wiping down everything with an old piece of cloth that he found on the floor. After a few hours he had the entire place wiped down and the sun was beginning to rise. Jacob covered up the window in the bedroom and he laid down to get some sleep.

John went up to down to the sheriff's office and found out that the property was abandoned. He went to the bank across the street and purchased the property under Charles's name. He knew no one would dare mess with the property if it was under someone's name that was highly respected.

After that was done he went back to the estate and began putting some of the Jacobs belongings into a crate. He planned to take them over to the house when the sun began to set. He wasn't sure what to do as far as food considering Jacobs current situation. He threw in a couple bottles of whiskey, just for fun.

John walked the estate grounds, making sure that everyone was working and keeping up with their daily tasks as usual. He had no idea what to expect from Charles's journey but if he did succeed and came home, everything would be as he would have wanted it. As it should be.

John had also noticed there were rumors circulating amongst the staff about why Charles was gone. A few said that he was killed by Cassandra and she chose to leave the estate to continue her reign of terror elsewhere. Others believed that Charles had killed Cassandra then began to travel to a far and holy place where he could imprison her remains. All he could do was reassure them that Charles did not die by Cassandra's hands and that he would be returning soon. He knew it was a hopeful scenario since he had no idea what was happening on the journey but it was better to hope for the best than assume the worst.

It had become dusk and John made his way to the newly purchased property. He noticed there was a dim glow coming from under the front door. He drew his pistol, slowly approached the door and knocked gently.

"John, put that pistol away and come inside." Jacob said with amusement.

"How did you know it was me and my pistol was drawn?" John asked Jacob in a shocked tone.

"Have you forgotten what I am? My senses are much stronger than any animal, so I heard you approaching and cocking the gun." Jacob chuckled.

"Right. That's something that will definitely take some getting used to. The property has been purchased and I brought you some of your belongings from the house." John said as he lifted the crate from the back of the wagon he was steering.

Jacob took the crate from John and carried it with ease as he saw John struggling to bring it in. "Thank you my friend. I appreciate all that you have done. I'm guessing you purchased it under Charles's name?" Jacob said as he sat the crate down in his room.

"Yes. I figured you wouldn't have any trouble that way. Plus, ummm…, I wasn't sure how to handle your meal situation." John stammered.

Jacob laughed. "John, I still eat regular food. I just need to feed on blood as well but I believe animal blood will suffice. I know this will be an odd and strange request but when the staff kill one of the cows, please have them collect the blood in jars for me. I'm sure there will be questions as to why they are doing that but maybe tell them it's per the town doctor's request. I doubt they will question that." Jacob felt ashamed to ask for such a gruesome thing but it was better than harming someone.

"Strange indeed. But I will do it. If you need anything else please don't hesitate to ask Jacob." John said as he began making his way back to the wagon.

"I could not ask for anything else. You have done so much for me already." Jacob looked down at the floor with a grim expression. "Hopefully I can find a way to not be so angry with Charles. Perhaps when he returns he and I will discuss what happened. There is a lot I need to say to him."

"Don't be so hard on him or yourself. It has been a dark time for all of us, we should begin to look to the future and forgive the past." John said as he climbed up into the wagon seat.

"Wise words John. Thank you again." Jacob closed the door as John rode away.

A few days had passed by and Jacob had not heard anything about Charles. He began to fear the worst had happened and Cassandra may have in fact won their battle. Jacob began to feel the anger building up inside of him. Since the sun was still down, he headed off to the woods to look for branches to shape into stakes. If she did succeed, he would be ready for her return and he would put up the fight of life. Jacob used his speed and jetted off.

When he returned two hours later he picked up a familiar scent. He dropped the stakes he had made and rushed to the front of the house. There was no one to be seen but he knew Charles had been there. He followed the scent of his dear friend and it led him to the saloon. He cautiously walked in, he saw Charles slowly and gingerly making his way up the stairs of the saloon. Jacob moved just enough to see a woman opening the door to a room. She had the look of relief, joy and love on her face as she saw Charles standing there.

Jacob sat down for a drink and he realized that the woman was the very same person he saw in the saloon the night Charles left. He smiled and finished his drink, he knew that that day they were both worried about the same person but for different reasons. He was happy for Charles. Unfortunately for him, his enhanced hearing was picking up some noise that he had no business hearing so he quickly left and returned to his house.

He gathered up the stakes that he had dropped and placed them into the small fireplace. He lit them on fire and the warmth washed over him like a comforting blanket. It was a relief and meant that he could live his life, no matter how long or short it would be, in peace. His anger towards

Charles drifted away and the fear that dwelled deep within

followed right behind the anger. For the first time in a long

time, he felt content with what his new life was. He stood

there watching the fire as every stake he carved turned into

smolder ash.

He slowly began walking to the estate. He would

surprise Charles and welcome him home. As Jacob

approached the estate he could see the lights on in

Charles's study. He went to the back of the estate to slip in

through the window in his old room. Jacob knew the staff

would recognize him and he wasn't sure if Charles had told

any of them about the events that unfolded. He slowly and

quietly made his way to Charles's study, he noticed an

unusual silence in the house.

What he saw broke his heart, Charles was sitting in

his chair and there was a silence in the room that could only

mean one thing. A tear rolled down Jacobs face as he

walked over to Charles, he placed his hand on Charles

chest to confirm what he already knew. Charles was now at

peace. Jacob knew the moment he began walking down the

hallway. He should have been able to hear Charles's heart

beating but he heard nothing.

"Good-bye Charles. I wanted to tell you that you have always been like a father to me. You treated me like a son when others wouldn't have easily dismissed me. You always showed me love and compassion even when you were hurting after…" Jacob stopped for a moment as the heartache began to overwhelm him. "I need you to know that none of this is your fault and I place no blame on you for Cassandra's actions. I was mad when you left me behind but I understand why you did. Tell my father that I said hello and that in every way possible, you kept your promise to him. Rest easy my friend, I will miss you and I love you." Jacob lowered his head and wiped the tears from his eyes.

Just then Jacob heard the front door opening and a female voice was calling for Charles, he could tell she was making her way closer to the study. The woman gasped as she entered the room.

"My apologies dear boy, you startled me. You must be Jacob, it's a pleasure to meet you. I'm Carolyn." Carolyn said, smiling until she looked at Charles.

"You know who I am?" He asked, confused since he had no idea who she truly was.

"Yes, Charles told me about you." Carolyn moved closer to Charles. "He's gone, isn't he?" She asked with tears rolling down her face.

"Yes. He is gone." Jacob said as he shared tears of sadness with Carolyn.

"He asked us both to be here at eight o'clock for dinner. I think he knew he was going to go tonight and he wanted us to meet so we wouldn't have to grieve alone. Good-bye my sweet Charles." She said as kissed him on the forehead.

"He…he what?" Jacob stuttered. "That must have been why he was at my house today." Jacob smiled as another tear fell to the floor. "I followed his scent to the saloon and saw him entering your room. It was then I remembered that the day he left was the first time I saw you. You were sitting at a table alone and you had a very worried look on your face." He said to her.

"Yes, I remember that day. I remember seeing you and your kind smile as you left the saloon. He and I were." She was stopped by Jacob.

"I know. When I saw him go to you earlier, I heard what was the beginning of something intimate and I left. I did not want to invade a private and personal moment nor did I want to hear it." Jacob chuckled.

"Oh.. Well, thank you for respecting our privacy. Perhaps we should call for John to summon the undertaker. It seems wrong to just let him sit here." Carolyn said to Jacob.

"Yes, I agree." Jacob noticed something different about her than when he last saw her.

Carolyn had noticed the look that Jacob had given her before they went downstairs. She went to find John as Jacob waited in the sitting room. She informed John of Charles's passing and she watched as the news hit him like a ton of bricks. He left to get the undertaker immediately.

Carolyn went over to where Jacob was sitting and sipping on a glass of whiskey. "I have to ask, what was the look you gave me as we left Charles's study?" She looked at him with curiosity.

"I'm assuming that since you know who I am, you also know that I am not normal." He said to her and he watched her nod in agreement. "You are different from the last time we saw each other, you have an aura to you that you didn't have before. I think you are pregnant." Jacob said to Carolyn. There was some uncertainty to his assumption but that was the only explanation he could find for her newly acquired condition.

"What? How could you know that? I haven't been with anyone for quite some time, no one other than Charles." Tears began to build up in the corners of her eyes.

"Carolyn, Charles was like a father to me and if you would allow it, I would like to watch over you and the baby. I have no other family and I would be honored if you would consider me as part of your family." Jacob smiled at her.

"The honor, Jacob, would be mine. I know Charles cared a great deal about you, especially to go to the lengths of keeping you back from the war he was preparing to face. He asked me for a specific mixture that would only make you sleep for a short time. It was much more diluted than what he used on her." She gave him a half smile then looked down at the floor.

"Thank you. For allowing me to be part of your family and for helping Charles keep me safe. From what I can tell, you are a kind woman. I can see why Charles liked you. I know the two of you would have been great together and amazing parents. I think I will make my way home and give you some time alone with Charles before the undertaker arrives." Jacob said to Carolyn as he glanced at Charles one last time.

"Thank you Jacob. I appreciate your kindness." Carolyn said as she knelt down next to Charles's chair.

Jacob left out of the front door, not worrying about being seen. The tears began to flow down his face as the weight of Charles's passing, he had felt as he did when he lost his father, Edward. He felt heartbroken, lost and alone. He tried to take comfort in Carolyn agreeing to take him in as family but the pain was still there. The pain was hit harder knowing that he would not be able to attend the funeral. He sighed as he entered his house and he sat on the edge of his bed. He knew it would be for a while and the only thing he could do was allow time to take its course.

He did just that, time passed and Carolyn had a beautiful baby boy. In remembrance, she named him after his father, Charles and gave him the middle name of Patrick after her father. Carolyn gave him the choice of what title he preferred when it came to the child growing up. He could be his older brother, uncle or a cousin, the only stipulation was that Jacob could never tell him about his curse or what truly happened to Charles along with Cassandra. Jacob didn't entirely agree with her decision but he respected it. She told Jacob that she just didn't want her child to grow up living in fear of the unknown.

As time went on, little Charles began to ask questions as he got older. Some questions about his father, as any child would have, but he also wondered why Jacob never looked any older. Jacob always responded with, "I guess I'm just lucky like that."

One day Jacob approached Carolyn with a somber expression. "Carolyn, I think it's time for me to go. Little Charles, who isn't so little anymore, is becoming more and more curious about why I'm not aging like you. My usual lines and stories are no longer satisfying his questioning. Plus, with you not wanting him to know more details about myself or his father, it's becoming more and more difficult to hide these facts." He looked sadly at the floor.

"Jacob, I am sorry that we have to keep those details quiet and I do understand what you're saying. I really wish you would stay here with us. We will be so sad to see you go and I know he will miss you dearly." Carolyn said to him.

"I will miss you both very much and this isn't something I want to do but I do think it's a smart decision. Perhaps when he's older I can return as a cousin that looks remarkably similar to his uncle Jacob." He snickered at the idea. "Also, to be honest, I feel I need to experience what life has to offer someone like me. I know I'm restricted to what I can do but I would like to learn as much as I can while I'm able to." Jacob gave her a halfhearted smile.

"We will always be here for you Jacob, you will always have a home and a family here that loves you. If you ever need anything, you come home. You promise me that." She said to him.

"Yes ma'am, I promise. If you ever need anything and John isn't able to help, leave a letter at my house. I may not be here with you both but I won't be far and I'll be home every now and then." Jacob said as he hugged her goodbye. "I'll return soon for a visit, until then take care of yourself and Charles."

"You keep yourself safe Jacob. Goodbye." She hugged him tightly and watched him walk out the door and into the night.

Jacob spent the next five years learning about the horrors of the world he was living in. He found out that there were more vampires out there than anyone could possibly imagine. There were stories of demons and witches that terrorized towns and villages but he never saw anything to prove their existence. He also encountered people who told strange and horrible stories of wolf-like creatures who were ferocious and walked on two legs like a man. They were mostly active during full moons, which Jacon thought was ridiculous and dismissed the tales.

That was until one night as he was making his way to a neighboring town, he heard a long and eerie howl. He looked up, noticing the full-moon, then he heard a deep menacing growl coming up behind him. He dismounted his horse, pulled his gun and aimed it in the direction of the beast that was stalking him. Out of the corner of his eye, he saw something charging at him. He turned and shot his gun in the direction of the animal but he missed. He holstered his gun and readied himself for a fight. His nails extended, his fangs lowered and he closed his eyes. He listened to the sounds around him until he found what he was searching for, the beating of a heart. It was incredibly fast and was approaching him just as quickly as it was beating. He opened his eyes just in time to catch the beast as it lunged at him and he threw it at a nearby tree. Jacob heard the sounds of its ribs breaking and gasping for air, that only lasted a moment. The beast was back on its feet, this time it looked at Jacob and ran off into the night. He stood there for a moment, waiting to see if the creature was going to return or not.

After a few more months of traveling Jacob decided it was time to head home. He had been gone for five years.

As he entered his home he noticed that there was a letter on the floor just inside of the door way. He picked it up and opened it. It was from Carolyn and he read it.

"Jacob,

I hope this letter finds you well. I am hoping that you will visit us soon, there is something I must speak with you about. Charles is doing well, he is excelling with his school and has made some great friends. John has been by often to check on us and make sure we have what we need. He has been keeping up with the daily tasks at the estate and has been running Charles's businesses. He said once my son is old enough he will make sure he learns the business so he can step into Charles's shoes as the head of the company. He has been quite the mentor to little Charles. Oh, and by the way he no longer wishes to be called Charles or little Charles, he wishes to be called Chuck. I'm not sure where he got that from but he likes it so we appease him. I hope to see you soon.

Sincerely,

Carolyn"

Jacob went straight over to the estate, he was filled with excitement and anticipation to see his family. He had been gone for so long that he had begun to really miss them. As he approached the estate, he was surprised to see how lit up everything was. He cautiously approached and looked into the windows, there were so many people inside the house and the mood seemed quite sad. He threw caution to the wind as he entered through the front door. Everyone stopped and stared as he made his way further into the room. He was looking for Carolyn and Charles but could not find either of them amongst the crowd of people. He did, however, see one familiar face.

"Excuse me sir, my name is Timothy. My uncle was Edward, he worked here a ways back but he always said that if I ever needed any work to come here and ask for a man by the name of John. Do you by chance know where I can find him?" Jacob said to John, while trying to keep a straight face.

"Hello Timothy, pleasure to meet you. I am John. I knew your uncle Edward, he was a great man and he is missed dearly. Let me introduce you to the owner of the estate. To be honest with you, you've come during a difficult time. Why don't you come with me so I can explain a bit more of what's been going on and we can see what kind of work is available for you." John motioned for Jacob to follow him.

Once they got to the kitchen, Jacob looked around to see if anyone had followed them. When he was sure no one was nearby, he stopped John and looked him in the eyes. "John, what's going on? Why are all these people here? Where are Carolyn and Charles?" He asked John frantically.

"It's good that you are home, Jacob. Or is it Timothy now?" John gave him a half smile.

"Nevermind that for now, please tell me what happened." Said Jacob with a more serious tone.

"I hate to have to tell you this but Carolyn has died. She became ill and it just hit her so hard. The doctors weren't able to help her nor did her concoctions that she would make for herself. She said, about a week ago, that she was going to leave you a letter asking you to come by whenever you came home. I didn't think the illness would take her that quickly. Charles, or Chuck as he now wants to be called, has been staying in his room. Perhaps a visit from you would help him while he grieves for his mother." John's voice cracked as he was talking about Carolyn's passing.

"I… I can't believe she's gone. I should have come home sooner and been here with them. I will have to explain to him why I told everyone my name is Timothy; I will do my best to honor Carolyn's wishes and not tell him about my curse." Jacob looked down sadly and took a breath. "Where is he?"

"He's in her room." John answered.

Jacob walked to Carolyn's room, knocked on the door and slowly opened it. "Chuck, are you in here?" Jacob knew he was but he wanted him to hear his voice.

"JACOB?" He yelled excitedly. "You're here." He ran over to Jacob and threw his arms around him. "She's gone Jacob, my mother is really gone. I keep expecting her to come walking through that door but I know she never will." Chuck collapsed to his knees and began crying.

"I know this is difficult but I understand your pain. Believe me when I say, it will get better and it will get easier. It'll just take some time. When I lost my parents, it hurt for a while. Even when I heard the news that your father was gone, it brought up all those feelings again plus the hurt of losing him. I know it doesn't feel like it'll ever go away but I promise you it will." Jacob could see the heartbreak in Chuck's eyes and it made his heart hurt even more for the boy.

Chuck wiped the tears from his eyes and looked up at Jacob. "Will you stay with us? I mean me. I have inherited this house and all the responsibility that comes with it, I am not quite ready for that kind of responsibility. Plus, soon I will be starting to work with John, so I can take over the family business. It is so much all at once and everyone is expecting me to just jump right in. I need help and I would really appreciate you being here with me." He pleaded with Jacob to stay.

"Of course I will stay. There is just one thing I need to ask. When I arrived here, I introduced myself as Timothy. Some people around town thought I died from an attack from a wild animal, this was long before you were born. So, to keep them from asking hundreds of questions, I made up a fake name. It has worked for me any time that I've been seen in town." Jacob smiled at Chuck, who was looking at him with a puzzled look. "I know it sounds strange but you can ask John about it, he will verify what I've said."

"I believe you, it's just that I swear you have not aged a day since you were last here. The only thing that I can tell that is different is your hair. How is that even possible?" Chuck asked him suspiciously.

"It must be all the traveling, I do a lot of walking and the fresh air keeps me looking young." A lie was the only answer Jacob could give him. Jacob knew that he wouldn't be able to stay for long because, like before he left, Chuck's curiosity would only grow and his questioning would just increase.

Chuck smiled and picked himself up off of the floor. "Ok, I guess we should go down and thank the guests for coming. Tomorrow will be a brand new day, I can begin healing and become a man my parents would be proud of." He began walking down the stairs and stopped at the bottom of the steps while everyone turned their attention to him. "Excuse me everyone, I would like to thank you all for coming out today to celebrate my mother's life and expressing your condolences. She was a kind, gentle woman and an absolutely incredible mother. I know she would be extremely grateful to you all for being here." Chuck said as he gave his guests a warm smile.

People started leaving after Chuck thanked them. The staff began cleaning up the house, once everyone had left, the only people still there were John, Jacob and Chuck. They sat by the fireplace, telling stories of Charles and Carolyn. Mostly filling in Jacob on events that had happened while he was gone. There were so many great and fun stories that Jacob had lost track of time. He glimpsed over and saw the sun beginning to rise. He excused himself from the table saying he was feeling tired and wanted to get some sleep. John and Chuck agreed with him that it was time to go to bed and get some rest.

Jacob laid there thinking about the tasks ahead of him. He didn't know how he could help Chuck, he wasn't very business savvy nor was he familiar with the process. He could propose to simply be an unseen advisor, that way he wouldn't take any credit away from his accomplishments but more than anything he felt like he would just be there for moral support. Aside from that he would be able to keep him safe from anyone with bad intentions. He laid there thinking it was nice to be able to sleep in a house with family. Jacob fell asleep after making sure the bedroom curtains were fully blocking out the sunlight.

Over the next two years, along with John, Jacob helped Chuck get the house staff in order and running smoothly. John already had a solid system in place for everyone, they used that as the foundation and made some minor adjustments. Even the staff commented on how well everything had been going. When it came to the business end, John was the primary person helping Chuck. Jacob began to feel useless, all the primary business duties happened during the day which made his ability to assist very limited. This went on for a few weeks, it came to a point where Jacob felt that it was time for him to leave. It would be hard for Chuck to understand why Jacob needed to leave, just like it was last time.

"Chuck, we need to have a talk." Jacob said to him in a monotone voice.

"You're leaving again, aren't you?" Chuck said to him.

"How did you know?" Jacob asked.

"I could tell that you've been thinking about it for about a week now." Said Chuck.

"You're right. I have been, but it's not a bad thing. You've grown so much over the time that I've been here. I can see that you don't need me around anymore and to be honest with you, I'm so proud of you." Jacob said to Chuck with a smile.

"I may not understand completely why you want to leave again but I do respect your decision. You have helped me a lot Jacob. Both emotionally and with things around here. You know you are always welcome here, this is your home." Chuck said to him.

"You're a great man Chuck. You're just like your parents, kind, warm hearted and a true gentleman. I know they are both as proud of you as I am, probably even more." Jacob stepped forward and gave him a hug.

"Thank you Jacob. That means a lot to me. Just promise me one thing." Chuck said to him with a smirk.

"Anything, you name it." Jacob replied with some curiosity.

"You will visit more than once every few years. You and John are the only family I have left." Chuck said as he hugged Jacob back.

"I promise I will visit often." Jacob smiled at Chuck.

Jacob left the estate and headed to his house north of town. He walked in, looked around and just smiled as he thought about Charles, Carolyn and his father. He had hoped that he made them proud, just like Chuck made him proud. It was a happy feeling that he basked like the warmth of the sun.

Jacob kept his promise and returned many times. He even went as far as adding dirt and flour in his hair to make himself look older. He told Chuck stories about a family he had and his son was born. Of course it was all made up, another cover story to allow him to watch over his family.

Jacob planned on keeping that promise for as long as he possibly could.

<u>**Carolyn**</u>

From the moment Charles left all she did was worry about him. Which initially seemed absurd to her since they barely knew each other, but there was something about him that she couldn't dismiss. There was this feeling that their paths were supposed to cross and that there was something planned for them. These feelings she knew better than to overlook, as her grandma always told her "Fate comes in the strangest of places and true love knows no limits."

The day he left for his voyage, she was in tears for hours. She did her best to keep the negative thoughts at bay but the harder she tried the stronger they became. She finally decided that perhaps a drink would soothe her nerves, at least enough so she could get some sleep. "The convenience of living above a saloon," she thought.

She went downstairs, ordered a double shot of whiskey and sat at a table alone. She sipped on her drink and savored the flavor after each sip. She watched a young gentleman entering the saloon. He had the look of someone who was hurting and filled with anger at the same time. She noticed that he was looking over at her, he must have recognized the look of dismay on her face. As he left the saloon, he gave her a final glance, they both smiled and nodded. It was as if they were acknowledging the others' pain.

As the next few days went by she would find herself thinking of Charles and she would begin to cry. She had hoped and prayed that he would be back already but her prayers remained unanswered. She would go on walks, hoping that nature and its beauty would calm her nerves. Unfortunately, all it did was deepen her worry.

One afternoon she heard a knock at her door. Knowing she had told the bartender she wasn't seeing any customers she yelled out, "I don't have any appointments today, come back next week." They knocked again. "Are you hard of hearing or can you not follow directions? I said.." She stopped and smiled when she opened the door to see Charles. She pulled him into the room and gave him the biggest hug. She let go when she heard him groan in pain. "What happened? Are you ok?"

"Hello to you too." He laughed. "I am ok, just a bit sore from the journey. I've missed you." He said as he pulled her in closer for a kiss.

Carolyn smiled. "I have missed you too." She said as she pulled him over to the bed.

They began kissing softly at first but the kisses became longer and deeper. She unbuttoned his shirt and gasped, his entire midsection was covered in a mix of deep purple, yellow and brown bruising. She gently kissed his rib cage, his back and made her way up to his neck. He turned around kissing her lips, her neck line and the top of her right shoulder.

This time there were no interruptions, no monsters to kill and no rushing. They finally shared the moment their bodies were aching for, the moment their souls craved for and the moment that their hearts beat for. Afterwards they laid there with her head resting on his chest. They savored the moment and Charles was finally free to be happy.

"Not to kill the mood but there are a few things I need to do today. With my previous situation now handled, there is someone I need to check on. Why don't you come by for dinner tonight at eight?" Charles loved the thought of spending more time with her but he could feel something was off inside of him. Maybe he was just exhausted from the journey, he wasn't sure.

"I would love that, I look forward to having dinner with you later. And maybe some dessert." She winked at him as he got up to get dressed. As he started putting his clothes back on Carolyn thought she noticed something odd with his bruising. She couldn't quite make it out because he was moving around too much.

Charles leaned over and kissed her. He smiled and kissed her again. "I can't wait to see you later, I miss you already." He said as he walked out of the door.

Her heart beat with joy as she began getting ready for dinner with Charles. In the back of her mind there was this strange feeling, this thought that something was wrong but she quickly dismissed it as paranoia. She readied herself and began making her way to his estate. She noticed that the sun had already begun to set and in a short while it would be nightfall.

When she arrived, she dismounted from her horse and one of the stable workers led it to the barn. She thanked him and made her way inside. There was a silence in the air that she found to be truly unsettling. The fire was roaring, giving off a comforting warmth but she did not see her love. She heard a creak from the floorboards upstairs, cautiously she made her way up.

She gasped as she entered the room. She saw a young man kneeling at Charles's and he quickly looked over at her. Before she could speak she looked at Charles and she could tell that he was finally at peace. The moonlight gave his face a pale glow as he sat in the chair in his study. He no longer looked in pain and he had a slight smile across his face. She looked at Jacob.

"My apologies dear boy, you startled me. You must be Jacob, it's a pleasure to meet you. I'm Carolyn." Carolyn said, smiling at him. The smile slowly faded as she looked back at Charles.

"You know who I am?" He asked with confusion.

"Yes, Charles told me about you." Carolyn moved closer to Charles. "He's gone, isn't he?" She asked with tears rolling down her face.

"Yes. He is gone." Jacob said as he shared tears of sadness with Carolyn.

"He asked us both to be here at eight o'clock for dinner. I think he knew he was going to go tonight and he wanted us to meet so we wouldn't have to grieve alone. Good-bye my sweet Charles." She said as kissed him on the forehead.

"He…he what?" Jacob stuttered. "That must have been why he was at my house today." Jacob smiled as another tear fell to the floor. "I followed his scent to the saloon and saw him entering your room. It was then I remembered that the day he left was the first time I saw you. You were sitting at a table alone and you had a very worried look on your face." He said to her.

"Yes, I remember that day. I remember seeing you and your kind smile as you left the saloon. He and I were." She was stopped by Jacob.

"I know. When I saw him go to you earlier, I heard what was the beginning of something intimate and I left. I did not want to invade a private and personal moment nor did I want to hear it." Jacob chuckled.

"Oh.. Well, thank you for respecting our privacy." She said to him as her cheeks turned red from embarrassment. "Perhaps we should call for John to summon the undertaker. It seems wrong to just let him sit here." Carolyn said to Jacob.

"Yes, I agree." Jacob noticed something different about her than when he last saw her.

She noticed the peculiar look that he had given her before they went downstairs. She went to find John as Jacob waited in the sitting room. She informed John of Charles's passing and she watched as the news hit him like a ton of bricks. He left to get the undertaker immediately.

She went over to where Jacob was sitting and sipping on a glass of whiskey. "I have to ask, what was the look you gave me as we left Charles's study?" She looked at him with curiosity.

"I'm assuming that since you know who I am, you also know that I am not normal." He said to her and he watched her nod in agreement. "You are different from the last time we saw each other, you have an aura to you that you didn't have before. I think you are pregnant." Jacob said to her. There was some uncertainty to his assumption but that was the only explanation he could find for her newly acquired condition.

"What? How could you know that? I haven't been with anyone for quite some time, no one other than

Charles." Tears began to build up in the corners of her eyes.

"Carolyn, Charles was like a father to me and if you would allow it, I would like to watch over you and the baby. I have no other family and I would be honored if you would consider me as part of your family." Jacob smiled at her.

"The honor, Jacob, would be mine. I know Charles cared a great deal about you, especially to go to the lengths of keeping you back from the war he was preparing to face. He asked me for a specific mixture that would only make you sleep for a short time. It was much more diluted than what he used on her." She gave him a half smile then looked down at the floor.

He thanked her for allowing him to become part of her family, she knew Charles would have wanted that and she could tell he was a kind and caring boy. Jacob left the estate so that she could have a final moment with Charles and say her good-byes to Charles in private.

She returned to Charles's side one last time. "My love, it seems you left me a gift before you departed from this world. I promise to love this child for the both of us and I will tell of the great man his father was. A kind, loving and brave man. Though, I will not tell him of the monsters that live in this world. I will keep that knowledge from him and protect him for as long as I live. I love you my dear, sweet Charles." She had tears rolling down her face as she spoke to him.

John had returned with the undertaker and his staff. They carried Charles's body out of the house with respect and gentleness. John walked over to Carolyn and handed her a letter that Charles had written for her before he passed.

"My dearest Carolyn,

If you're reading this then I have succumbed to my injuries from my voyage. I am glad we were able to share a moment together, a moment where our love was all that mattered. If not for you, I would not have been able to make it home and I don't mean because of the sedative you gave me. Yes, that helped immensely but my thoughts of you are what truly kept me alive. You gave me the strength to make it home, the courage to do what had to be done and your love guided me to your door. I know the coming days will be difficult. I hope that you and Jacob can grieve together and push

through the sadness of my passing. He is a
great man and he is like a son to me. One of
my regrets is that I didn't have any children
to carry on my family name and to share my
love with.

I have instructed John to speak to my
lawyer and fulfill my last wish. I am leaving
you my home and all that I own. What was
once mine is now yours. All I ask in return
is that you help Jacob whenever he is in
need. He is a proud boy but he will be
limited to a life in the shadows and it will be
difficult for him. John will instruct the staff
that you are now the head of the house and
they will treat you as good as they treated
me. They are like my extended family.

I'm sorry I won't be there to enjoy
the rest of your days with you. My biggest
regret is that I didn't meet you sooner in life.
I know I could have been a great husband to
you and shown you a life filled with so
much happiness and love. In such a short
time, you showed me what real love truly is

and I am eternally grateful for that. I love
you now and forever.

Love,

Charles."

Carolyn was in tears from his letter. She knew that
he would have made an amazing father and incredible
husband. She walked over to where John was sitting in the
dining room and sat across from him.

"John, according to Jacob, I am pregnant. I can say
with unwavering certainty that Charles is the father. I may
reside above a saloon but I am not a worker there." She
said to John.

"Ma'am, I have no reason to doubt you and I know
Jacobs' senses are much stronger than a regular person's. I
am here for whatever you may need. As the pregnancy
progresses I will make certain that a nursery is prepared for
the baby." John said to her as he sipped a drink he had
poured himself. "If you don't mind, I will prepare the
funeral arrangements for Charles and see that he is buried
next to his parents and miss Chloe."

"Thank you John. I appreciate you and your help.
This is all so much to take in, in one evening. In one day. I
will return to my room at the saloon for tonight and if
possible tomorrow can we bring my belongings here? I

don't have much to bring over to be honest with you." Carolyn said as she began to tear up again.

"Yes ma'am, first thing in the morning, a couple of the staff and I will come over and load up the wagon.

The next morning all of Carolyn's belongings were brought over to the house. She looked around the estate in awe, never in her wildest dreams did she ever think she'd live in a place like that. The rooms were massive compared to her little room she was renting over the saloon.

The next nine months were filled with morning sickness, doctor visits and preparations for the baby. The day finally came and the baby was born without any complications. Carolyn was so happy when the doctor announced she had given birth to a healthy baby boy. He was eight pounds, nineteen inches long and had piercing blue eyes. She knew immediately what she was going to name him, Charles after his father and his middle name would be Patrick after her father. Of course, he would share Charles's last name and carry on the namesake for his family.

"You have given him a fine, strong name, Carolyn. He is a beautiful baby." Jacob said to her as he held the baby gently in his arms.

"Thank you, Jacob." She said.

"I agree. Why don't you get some rest Carolyn? I'll have the nanny come in and keep an eye on the baby. We'll wake you for his feeding." John said to her.

"Thank you both so much. I truly appreciate all of the help. I think I will rest briefly before the baby needs his feeding." Carolyn instantly fell asleep.

She was awoken by the sounds of a crying baby. She looked over and saw that John was just about to touch her shoulder to wake her up. She sat up and smiled as the nanny brought baby Charles over to her. She carefully brought him close and his crying stopped instantly. She began breastfeeding him and he fell asleep as he drank. She lovingly gazed down at her sweet baby and smiled at the thought that a part of Charles would always be with her.

Time went by quickly after the birth of the baby. His first word was mama, then he began crawling and then walking. Before she knew it he was running around the estate and exploring so many things. He was an active little boy and she was so happy with him. Thankfully she always had Jacob and John to help her with the baby, Charles's business and anything that needed to be done around the estate.

One day, shortly after Charles's seventh birthday, Jacob came to her expressing his concerns about Charles's inquisitive nature. The boy was smart and he was noticing things about his "uncle" Jacob that were very different from his mother and John. Jacob felt it was time to leave the estate and go out on his own. He needed to grow, in his own sense, and he felt bad for always having to lie to Charles about why he never looked any older or would only be around during the nighttime. She accepted his reasoning and reminded him that he always had a home and family to come back to, when he was ready or wanted to visit. Jacob was grateful and departed.

"Mama, where did Uncle Jacob go?" Charles asked her with some sadness in his voice.

"Well sweetie, he had to go and take care of some business. He asked me to tell you that he's going to miss you but he will come back to visit us as often as he can." She told him. She was hoping to reassure him that Jacob wouldn't be gone forever.

"I'm going to miss him too." Charles said sadly.

About a year had passed since Jacob left and one morning after breakfast Charles was running around the house and he ran up to Carolyn asking, in an excited tone, "Can we go outside and play mama?"

"Of course we can, put your shoes on and we can go explore the woods." She said to him as he ran to his room.

They didn't go too far, since there was a heavily wooded area not too far from the back of the estate. They ran around the trees and came to one that had something very odd on one of the branches. Charles looked up at a branch that had a round wooden lid-like object sitting on the branch.

"What's that mama?" Charles asked with a curious tone.

"I don't know, baby. Looks like someone made a place to sit in the tree. Maybe your daddy put it there for hunting deer or other animals. We can ask Mr. John about it later when we see him." She said as she stared at the strange seat.

"Ok. Want to race to that tree?" He asked her as he pointed at a tree in the distance.

"Ok. Let's race. On the count of three we'll run as fast as we can to the tree." She began counting. "One. Two. Thr…" Before she could say three he began running to the tree and she ran after him. "Hey, you didn't wait for me to say three." She said with a chuckle.

He let out a loud giggle. "I get a head start because I'm littler than you." He said, still giggling.

She let him win and smiled as he began jumping up and down bragging that he won.

"I won mama. I'm getting fast, aren't I?" He asked her with a big smile.

"Yes, you sure are." She said to him, she felt strange and winded. They hadn't run very far and she didn't go too fast, yet she felt as if she was running a marathon. She leaned against the tree and tried to catch her breath.

"Are you ok mama?" Charles asked with concern in his little voice.

"Of course, I am. You're just so fast and I need to catch my breath so I can catch you next time." She said to him as she stood up and began to breathe at a calmer pace.

"WOW!" He exclaimed. "Look at this tree mama, it looks like a bear scratched it." He said pointing at a tree where had previously left some deep and menacing claw marks.

She began to feel uneasy looking at the tree. She remembered the story Charles told her about Cassandra when she tried to kill Jacob. "Lets head back sweetie. It's almost time for lunch." She said to him nervously.

"Want to race back home?" He asked her.

"Maybe next time, let's enjoy our walk together. If we take our time, maybe you can catch a caterpillar." She said hoping to entice him to go slow for the walk back home.

"Ok. I hope I can catch two of them. One for you and one for Uncle Jacob for when he comes to see us." He said as he began looking at the ground and trees to find his prize.

"I'm sure he'd like that very much." She said to him as she looked around the area with caution.

When they returned home they had some lunch and Charles went up to his room to take a nap. After Carolyn was sure he was asleep she went to find John. He was in the kitchen giving one of the staff a list of items to pick up for the pantry and to have on hand for Carolyn and Charles.

"Excuse me John, may I speak to you when you have a moment." She said to him.

"Of course, I was just finishing up with the grocery list. What can I do for you?" He asked her with a smile.

"Charles and I were out for a walk earlier and we came across a tree that looked to have been scratched by some animal or ummm…" She was having difficulty saying what she thought made the marks.

"Or by Cassandra? Yes, your thinking is correct." He said to her.

"Oh. I was afraid of that. Charles thought it was done by a bear, which I was happy to let him think. I just wanted to know for sure, thank you." She looked down at the floor and began to feel dizzy. She grabbed her head with her right hand and reached out for John with her left hand as she began to lose her balance.

John quickly grabbed her hand and led her to a chair in the kitchen. "Carolyn, are you ok?" He asked as he helped her to sit down in the chair safely.

"I… I don't know. I was having difficulty catching my breath earlier, now this dizziness. Will you help me to my room and call for the doctor please?" She asked him in a soft and worried tone.

"Absolutely. I'll have him come see you right away." He said as he slowly walked with her up the stairs and into bed.

The doctor arrived and began his assessment of Carolyn. She had no fever, no cough or any other physical symptoms.

"As far as I can tell, you are a perfectly healthy woman. I think you are just suffering from exhaustion. It's possible that you just over exerted yourself which would cause your shortness of breath and dizziness. I recommend you get some rest and increase your fluid intake. A few days of that as you should be feeling as good as new." He said as he put his equipment back into his bag.

Carolyn looked at the doctor displeased with his assessment. "That's all? Exhaustion? Thank you for your time doctor." She said to him sarcastically.

John walked the doctor out and returned to Carolyn, who was now accompanied by Charles in her bed. "Is there anything I can get you?" He asked her. He assumed that she wouldn't want to discuss seeing the doctor in front of her son.

"No thank you John but thank you for your help." She was indeed annoyed with the doctor and his ridiculous assessment. She knew something was wrong but she just didn't know what.

As time passed Charles got older and she got sicker. She saw the doctor frequently and he was never able to figure out what was wrong with her. This went on for three years, she had good days and some bad ones. On the bad ones she was unable to get out of bed for most of the day but on the good ones she was filled with energy and life.

Towards the end of the year some strange and terrifying things began happening.

On the anniversary of the death of his father, Charles asked if they could go and visit his grave. He wanted to say hi and leave some flowers for his sister Chloe. Though he never met her, he was adamant on calling her his big sister and showed love for her. Carolyn was happy to oblige her sweet son and agreed to the visit. They made a quick trip to the town's florist and picked up some flowers, Charles was insisting on picking them out himself.

When they arrived at the burial grounds, they were both in shock and horrified at what they saw. Charles's headstone was knocked over and completely destroyed. It had been smashed into pieces and scattered all over the ground. It even looked as if something had tried digging into the ground. Chloe's headstone was knocked over and was laying on the ground broken in half. The ground looked the same, dirt everywhere and again like something was digging towards the coffin.

"Why would someone do something so horrible to their graves?" Charles asked with anger in his voice.

"I don't know Charles. I really don't know. This breaks my heart, I am so sorry sweetie." Carolyn said with tears running down her face.

She watched as her son placed the flowers on Chloe's broken headstone and he turned and ran back to the house. Something odd caught her eye as she looked back at Charles's shattered headstone. There was one piece that was larger than the rest, the part that had his first name on it.

She struggled to kneel down and examine the chuck of stone. She gasped when she noticed there was blood and scratch marks over his name. With the little strength that she had she flipped over the price to follow the blood stains on the rock.

Every hair on her arms stood up, her entire body shuddered and she was chilled to the bone with what she saw.

There were words carved into the broken headstone. They read "revenge will be mine."

Carolyn stood up as fast as she could, she stumbled over feet as she made her way back to the house. She slammed the door shut and locked it as quickly as she could. She yelped as she turned around to see John walking up behind her.

"What has happened? Charles came running in here upset and slamming his bedroom door. Now you enter and slam this door and lock it as if something was chasing you?" John said with suspicion and worry.

She told him what happened and what the stone had carved into it. She looked up at him with fear in her eyes. "Is it possible that… that she's still alive? That he failed all those years ago or she fooled him and finally found her way back?" Carolyn asked John frantically.

"He was quite sure that the job was completed." John said as he looked at Carolyn with fear. "But I don't know how these things work, can a monster like that truly die and stay dead? I don't know Carolyn." He said with a tremble in his voice.

"What do we John? Jacob is not here and I haven't heard from him in a while. Wha…" Carolyn collapsed to the floor.

"Carolyn. Carolyn, wake up." John shouted.

Charles came rushing down the stairs and almost tripped over the last few steps. "What happened? Is she ok?" He asked terrified that she was dead.

"She'll be fine. Let's get her up to bed." John said to him as they stopped her up and carried her upstairs.

A few hours later Carolyn woke up. Charles was laying in bed next to her and he was sound asleep. She slipped out of bed, went to Charles's old writing desk and wrote a letter for Jacob. When she finished she called for one of the staff to fetch John. He came right away.

"What is it, are you ok?" He asked her.

"I'll be fine but I need a favor. Please take this letter to Jacobs house and slide it under the door. I've asked him to come home but I don't know when he'll see it. Hopefully before anything bad happens."

"I will deliver it right away. Please try and rest Carolyn." John said to her as he helped her back into bed.

The next couple of months were difficult for her. Her illness had progressed, the doctors still had no diagnosis or any idea about what was going on with her. She had pulled out her potions and elixir, making concoctions that she believed would help her. For about a week and a half they did help, especially when the pain began to really get severe.

Some nights she would wake up with a feeling that she was being watched. She'd light a lantern but never saw anything or anyone. There would be tapping at the windows and every couple of nights someone would be pounding on the front door. No one was ever seen when the door would be opened by the staff. During one particular storm she could have sworn she saw the silhouette of a person against the wall when the lightning would flash.

Carolyn called for John once more. "Have you heard anything from Jacob? I fear the end is near for me and I need him to help keep Charles safe." She coughed into her handkerchief.

"No, I'm sorry. I have not heard anything from him. Hopefully we hear something soon." John tried not to look her directly in the eyes. He did not want her to see the concern he had growing in his mind. She looked so frail and weak, it broke his heart to think that poor Charles would grow up without his mother soon.

"I'm not dead yet, John. Stop looking so sad and mournful." She chuckled, trying to get a laugh out of him.

"My apologies. Can I bring you anything? Perhaps soup or water?" He asked her.

"Not right now. I think I will sleep some more. Hopefully I'll have the strength to join you and Charles for dinner." She said as she closed her eyes to sleep.

She woke up when she heard Charles talking to John in the hallway. "Charles, come here my love." She called out to him.

"Mom, I have asked you to stop calling me that and please call me Chuck. How are you feeling?" He asked as he climbed into bed next to her.

"I'm sorry Chuck. I forget, you're not so little anymore." She snickered. "I'm feeling fine, love. What were you talking to John about?" she asked him.

"We were discussing what to have for dinner. I told him a soup would be best, something easy for you to eat and enjoy." He said to her.

"Oh really? That's all you two were talking about?" She raised an eyebrow at him.

"I was also asking him how he thought you were doing. You keep saying fine but I can tell that you're not telling me the truth. I'm just worried about you." He said emotionally.

"My sweet boy, you don't have to worry about me. I'm sure I'll be feeling better soon enough." She knew that meant she would be gone soon to be with his father, but she wanted to comfort her son. "I love you so much Charles, I mean Chuck. I am so proud of the young man you are becoming and how smart you are. I know your father would be so incredibly proud of you as well." She smiled but started to cough again.

"Don't talk like that, it feels like you're saying goodbye. I'm not ready for that. I need you here with me. I forbid you to die and leave me here." He said, trying to sound authoritative while being sincere.

"Yes sir. You have forbidden me to die so I will stay right here with you." She winked at him and made him smile.

"Good. Now get some rest and I will bring you up some soup when it is ready. We're having the cook make chicken soup just for you." He said to her smiling as he walked over to the door of the room.

"Mmm, my favorite kind of soup. I will look forward to a nice big bowl of that." She licked her lips in a comical manner and smiled.

She turned over to get some more sleep. His words made her happy and fell asleep with a smile on her face.

She woke up again a moment later and saw nothing but darkness. She looked around trying to see but could not see anything at all. Then everything came into focus. She was on a white sandy beach, waves were crashing into shore and the mist from the waves falling gently on her face. She smiled and embraced the cool feeling. She began walking in the sand, noticing she was barefoot and enjoying the warmth on her toes.

She thought that it was strange to wake up on a beach she had never seen before and one that was completely deserted. She continued walking and started to wonder if she was in heaven. It was so calm and tranquil. She wasn't in any pain, felt amazing and healthy. She wondered if she was going to see her beloved Charles walking up to her soon.

"He's not here." She heard a woman's voice say from behind her.

She jumped and turned around to see someone she had never met before. "Excuse me. You startled me. Who isn't here?" She asked the strange woman.

The woman smiled. "Charles. He's not here. It's only you and me, Carolyn." Said the woman.

There was a strange and sinister tone in the woman's voice that gave Carolyn the chills. "How do you know who I was looking for? How do you know my name?" she asked nervously.

"I know a lot more than just your name. I know you live in his old home, and you bore his child." The woman said to Carolyn.

"How do you know all that?" Carolyn said as she began trembling with fear.

The woman laughed. "I know something else, you will never see your son again." She said as her face bore an evil snare and she stared intensely at Carolyn.

Carolyn turned and began running as fast as she could in the sand. Her feet kept slipping with each step she took. When she thought she was a safe distance from her attacker she looked back and stopped running. There was no one in sight. She walked over to an area that several large logs and a fire roaring. She embraced the warmth for a moment until she heard footsteps coming up behind her. Carolyn was frozen with fear.

The stranger whispered something in Carolyn's ear before she grabbed her from behind. Carolyn struggled against the woman while she dragged her over to the water. Carolyn could feel each hit of the waves as they slammed into the pair. As she was pulled deeper and deeper into the water, Carolyn fought with all of her strength. She was no match for this woman. Soon the water was above both of their heads and still the stranger dragged her further and further into the depths of the water. They were so far out that it was now pitch black.

Carolyn could feel her lungs fighting for air bit with each gasp she only gulped down a mouthful of water. She knew she could not win, and she gave into the darkness. Her eyes fluttered open, then closed and finally closed for the last time. In the back of her mind, she could hear someone calling out to her.

It was her son and John. They yelled her name, she could feel their hands on hers, but it was too late. She was gone.